Gabe ... Jessi, and ... She was that much a part of him now.

"Ever thought about living in Washington?" Gabe's question just asked itself, leaving him as startled as Jessi appeared to be when she glanced over her shoulder at him.

"You mean make our marriage legal?" Jessi sounded shocked.

"Surely the thought has crossed your mind."

"Maybe," Jessi murmured, confessing nothing.

"Admit it, Jessi," Gabe said. "You've thought about what it would be like to be married to me, probably more than once."

"And if I have?"

"What did you decide?"

"You're a good man, Gabe. You appreciate the worth of family. I think you'd make a great husband."

"*Your* husband?" Gabe couldn't resist asking....

the leather seat and stood on the driver's side, arms outstretched to Gabe. He assisted her to the ground via an

Dear Reader,

July brings you the fifth title of Silhouette Romance's VIRGIN BRIDES promotion. This series is devoted to the beautiful metaphor of the traditional white wedding and the fairy-tale magic of innocence awakened to passionate love on the wedding night. In perennial favorite Sandra Steffen's offering, *The Bounty Hunter's Bride*, a rugged loner finds himself propositioned by the innocent beauty who'd nursed him to health in a remote mountain cabin. He resists her precious gift…but winds up her shotgun groom when her father and four brothers discover their hideaway!

Diana Whitney returns to the Romance lineup with *One Man's Promise*, a wonderfully warmhearted story about a struggling FABULOUS FATHER and an adventurous single gal who are brought together by their love for his little girl and a shaggy mutt named Rags. And THE BRUBAKER BRIDES are back! In *Cinderella's Secret Baby*, the third book of Carolyn Zane's charming series, tycoon Mac Brubaker tracks down the poor but proud bride who'd left him the day after their whirlwind wedding, only to discover she's about to give birth to the newest Brubaker heir….

Wanted: A Family Forever is confirmed bachelor Zach Robinson's secret wish in this intensely emotional story by Anne Peters. But will marriage-jaded Monica Griffith and her little girl trust him with their hearts? Linda Varner's twentieth book for Silhouette is book two of THREE WEDDINGS AND A FAMILY. When two go-getters learn they must marry to achieve their dreams, a wedding of convenience results in a *Make-Believe Husband*…and many sleepless nights! Finally, a loyal assistant agrees to be her boss's *Nine-to-Five Bride* in Robin Wells's sparkling new story, but of course this wife wants her new husband to be a *permanent* acquisition!

Enjoy each and every Silhouette Romance!

Regards,

Joan Marlow Golan

Joan Marlow Golan
Senior Editor Silhouette Books

Please address questions and book requests to:
Silhouette Reader Service
U.S.: 3010 Walden Ave., P.O. Box 1325, Buffalo, NY 14269
Canadian: P.O. Box 609, Fort Erie, Ont. L2A 5X3

MAKE-BELIEVE HUSBAND
Linda Varner

Silhouette
ROMANCE™
Published by Silhouette Books
America's Publisher of Contemporary Romance

This book is dedicated to
Dr. Annette Meador and her wonderful nurses.
Thanks for keeping me writing!

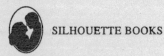 SILHOUETTE BOOKS

ISBN 0-373-19310-6

MAKE-BELIEVE HUSBAND

Copyright © 1998 by Linda Varner Palmer

This edition published by arrangement with Harlequin Books S.A.

® and TM are trademarks of Harlequin Books S.A., used under license. Trademarks indicated with ® are registered in the United States Patent and Trademark Office, the Canadian Trade Marks Office and in other countries.

Printed in U.S.A.

Books by Linda Varner

Silhouette Romance

Heart of the Matter #625
Heart Rustler #644
The Luck of the Irish #665
Honeymoon Hideaway #698
Better To Have Loved #734
A House Becomes a Home #780
Mistletoe and Miracles #835
As Sweet as Candy #851
Diamonds Are Forever #868
A Good Catch #906
Something Borrowed #943
Firelight and Forever #966
*Dad on the Job #1036
*Believing in Miracles #1051
*Wife Most Unlikely #1068
†Won't You Be My Husband? #1088
†Mistletoe Bride #1193
†New Year's Wife #1200
‡Corporate Groom #1280
‡Make-Believe Husband #1310

*Mr. Right, Inc.
†Home for the Holidays
**Three Weddings and a Family

LINDA VARNER

confesses she is a hopeless romantic. Nothing is more thrilling, she believes, than the battle of wits between a man and a woman who are meant for each other but just don't know it yet! Linda enjoys writing romance and considers herself very lucky to have been both a RITA finalist and a third-place winner in the National Readers' Choice Awards in 1993.

A full-time federal employee, Linda lives in Arkansas with her husband and their two children. She loves to hear from readers. Write to her at 813 Oak St., Suite 10A-277, Conway, AR 72032.

SAMPSON FAMILY TREE

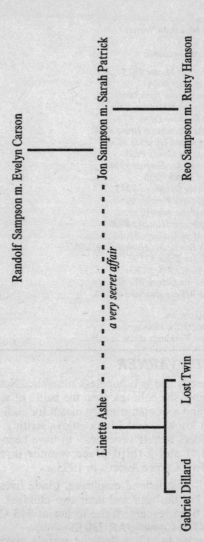

Randolf Sampson m. Evelyn Carson

Jon Sampson m. Sarah Patrick

Reo Sampson m. Rusty Hanson

Linette Ashe - - - *a very secret affair*

Gabriel Dillard

Lost Twin

Chapter One

"Jessica Landers, do you take Gabriel Dillard to be your husband?"

"I do," Jessi said, her gaze locked with that of her blue-eyed, brown-haired groom, a disconcertingly handsome male she'd met for the first time mere hours ago. Dressed in his suede jacket, denim jeans, and boots, he looked like one gorgeous hunk of mountain man. Jessi tried to picture herself cooking up some *vittles* for him over an open flame.

She couldn't. Was that an omen?

"And do you, Gabriel, take Jessica to be your wife?"

"I do."

His gaze swept Jessi from top to bottom and back up again, not missing a curve. Flustered by the appraisal, Jessi glanced away and instantly spied, of all things, the door.

Could she still escape?

Should she?

Unsure, she looked back at Dillard, who now stared at the octogenarian preacher who'd so graciously agreed to perform their Saturday-night wedding.

Desperate to affirm that she wasn't making the biggest

mistake in her thirty—almost thirty-one—years, Jessi stole
the moment to study Dillard's profile. Surely there were
hints of character there, she thought, at once noting the
telltale dimple in his cheek. Companion to the wicked twinkle in his eye, it promised a crooked sense of humor even
as the set of his nose and chin promised bullheaded stubbornness.

"Are there rings?"

"Oh, um, yes," Jessi replied, tugging from her thumb
the ring she'd purchased for Dillard that afternoon. She
wondered if her rugged groom had remembered to buy one,
a worry proved needless when he immediately dug into an
inside pocket of his jacket. Jessica guessed he'd bought a
plain gold band like the one she'd purchased for him. Not
knowing his personal tastes really had narrowed her
choices.

"Exchange the rings, please."

With hands that trembled as badly as the old reverend's,
Jessi slipped the circle of gold onto Dillard's third finger,
left hand. He then did the same to her, his large hands
steady, his touch electric. Jessi didn't give the marriage
token so much as a glance, so rattled was she by that brief
but disconcerting contact.

His good looks and blatant masculinity could prove
damned distracting during their marriage of convenience,
she realized with some dismay—just one of many reasons
to get the hell out of Sacramento before it was too late.

Or was *he* really the problem? she then asked herself. In
truth, weren't three years' worth of celibacy more to blame
for tonight's sweaty palms and hammering heart?

But of course, she reassured herself. These lonely days,
even Frankenstein had sex appeal....

At that moment, the preacher murmured approval of their
cooperation thus far, a sound that barely penetrated Jessi's
daze of indecision. "Now face one another and, in unison,
repeat after me—with this ring I promise to be your partner...."

Jessi automatically echoed the words she'd agreed to mere hours ago, noting with much embarrassment how breathless she sounded now compared to Dillard's resonant bass. No doubt the witnesses to tonight's ceremony—Elaina Rivera of Rivera Employment Agency, and the preacher's wife, name forgotten—could hear the tremor.

"I will respect, trust and care for you…"

"'I will respect, trust and care for you…'"

"From this day, forever."

Forever? Jessi's heart stopped. The word was *forth.* She'd written it herself. Was the old man ad-libbing or just too blind to read? Confused, Jessi darted a glance at Dillard, who, for the first time that night, looked a little bemused himself.

"From this day forever…." the bespectacled reverend patiently prompted, obviously used to nervous brides and grooms who forgot their lines.

Jessi swallowed convulsively. Short of making a scene that might alert this man of God to their unusual circumstances—namely, the fact that there was no chance of a forever between them—she had no choice but to repeat the line. Clearly Dillard came to the same conclusion at the same instant, for in unison they made a vow that neither intended to keep.

"'From this day forever….'"

The preacher smiled. "By the powers invested in me by the state of California this fifteenth day of October, I pronounce you man and wife." As though this was his favorite part of the ceremony, he took off his glasses and beamed at Dillard. "You may kiss the bride."

So here it was…the intimacy she'd dreaded ever since she'd first laid eyes on him that morning. The butterflies in Jessi's stomach fluttered wildly, the culmination of a week's worth of prevarication, no doubt. Determined not to embarrass herself and Dillard by recoiling, she squared her shoulders and stood her ground as her husband stepped forward. Instead of kissing her, however, he reached out, grabbed her right hand and pumped it vigorously up and down.

"This is great…perfect. Thanks a million." The next instant, Dillard released her to shake hands with the startled man who'd just married them.

Immediately, Elaina rushed forward to offer congratulations and, no doubt, distract the preacher and his frowning wife. Jessi, feeling shockingly cheated by the unexpected handshake, barely noticed. There followed a lecture on filing the license at the courthouse on Monday to make everything legal, after which Dillard paid the preacher for services rendered. He then scooped up his cowboy hat from a pew and hustled Jessi and Elaina out of the tiny chapel, a picturesque structure in the heart of the busy city.

On a rush of night air came a momentary lift of spirits that was mostly due to relief. It was over. Done. She was well and truly married…at least for now. The bad of it was that she had a husband who made her damned nervous. The good was that a few weeks' worth of high adventure in the form of a treasure hunt lay ahead, not to mention a hefty salary.

Since the good far outweighed the bad—the man had furnished *ten* references, after all—there was definitely a rainbow stretched across yesterday's bleak horizon. And in the pot at the end of it waited more than enough money to pay back her student loans and put a down payment on a house.

Then she'd find a good location and start her own catering business or maybe open a neighbourhood café or something.

"Dinner is my treat," Elaina announced when they paused under the overhang of the porch roof, adding, "That is, if you two don't have other plans…?"

"Actually, I wasn't sure how long all this would take, so I told my sitter I'd be late," Jessi replied. Anna Kate, her four-year-old daughter, was home in their Highlands, California, apartment with the teenaged girl who kept her when Jessi worked nights—too often this past year. Since those two always had a ball together, neither would mind if Jessi and her new husband...Oh God...dined with the woman whose ingenuity had brought them together.

"Gabe?" Elaina, an innovative employment contractor of national reputation, had turned to the groom.

"No plans," he said, finger combing his shaggy brown hair and then settling his hat just so on his head.

"Good. The two of you have a nine o'clock reservation at Chateau en Espagne right up the street, there."

"You mean you're not going, too?" Jessi blurted in a panic.

"No, dear," Elaina said, giving her shoulder a reassuring pat. "You and Gabe may have memorized one another's résumés and vital statistics, but you still need time alone to get better acquainted. Much is at stake here for all of us. I want everything to go off without a hitch when you meet August Taylor on Monday afternoon."

"Actually," Dillard drawled, "'a hitch' is exactly why we're here tonight, isn't it?"

"So it is," Elaina agreed. Laughing, she reached for the marriage certificate he held and tucked it into her purse. "I'll just take this, if you don't mind. Promised I'd fax a copy to our employer tonight. I'll give it back so you can make everything legal before you leave town Monday morning."

Gabe shook his head slowly from side to side as though vastly amused by the whole situation. Jessi wished she could feel as lighthearted about everything. Unfortunately, reality had dawned and her rainbow dimmed correspondingly.

What on earth have I done?

"Now the restaurant is just a block south...see those twinkling lights there? They're expecting you." Elaina hugged Dillard hard, then stepped up to Jessi and did the same. "Relax, honey," she whispered before releasing her. "This is only for three weeks, four tops. Think of the money and remember I personally checked for a criminal record. This man is so clean I was half tempted to marry him, myself. Unfortunately I can't cook.''

Jessi nodded numbly. In seconds, she and Dillard stood alone.

''Shall we?'' he asked, offering her his hand and a smile.

Swallowing hard, Jessi accepted both, and with fingers lightly laced, they headed down the path to the sidewalk. She felt awkward and uncomfortable, as though she'd worn shoes that didn't match and was trying to keep everyone from noticing.

Undoubtedly this resulted from the fact that he was so easy on the eyes—something for which she'd not been prepared. It didn't help that her companion didn't appear the least bit perturbed about anything. And when he began to whistle the ''Wedding March'' under his breath, she stopped short and glared at him.

''Oh, Mr. Dillard, must you?'' The sacrilege appalled her.

''Second thoughts?''

Jessi, who wanted to know the answer to that question herself, gave it serious consideration before replying. ''Actually, I'm way past seconds and almost through thirds.''

''But I assumed you were okay with this.''

''I am…was…am.'' She sighed. ''I guess I just don't know how to act around you.''

''If you promise to call me Gabe,'' he said, ''I'll share my plan of action.''

So he wasn't one hundred percent comfortable with this, either. Oddly enough, that made Jessi feel a little better.

''Okay…Gabe.''

He glanced back the way they'd come, and, with a grunt of confirmation, turned to lead her to a stone bench on the narrow lawn of the chapel. It lay in shadow, protected from the glow of the streetlight by an oak tree. Gabe motioned for her to sit, then did the same without releasing her hand.

''All you have to do is pretend that you and I have just

landed the leads in the biggest, best adventure movie of the year. August Taylor is the producer, the director, the cameraman and the crew. Whenever he's around, we're a married couple in charge of an expedition trying to find lost treasure. I'm the hero, also known as the trusty guide. You're the heroine, also known as the beautiful cook.''

Beautiful?

''The rest of the time, we can be ourselves—a search and rescue guide with big dreams and a…?'' Obviously he waited for her to fill in the blank.

''Financially overextended chef with a dependent child.''

''Exactly. We're co-workers who recognize that opportunities to earn this kind of money don't come along except once in a lifetime and so we don't mind signing an inconsequential partnership agreement—''

''The marriage license…?''

Gabe nodded. ''—if that's what it takes to make this happen. Now are you feeling better about the whole thing now?''

''Sort of, but—''

''You have other questions.'' It was a statement of fact. Jessi detected no impatience in his tone.

''Frankly, yes, a few other questions have popped into my head.''

''Ask them. We have fifteen minutes to spare.''

''Okay.…'' She took a deep breath and selected one of the many queries tumbling about unanswered in her head. ''For one thing, I'm still a little confused about my role in all this. Why can't August Taylor's wife just make you guys some sandwiches or something when you get hungry? For that matter, why can't you make your own? Anyone— including my four-year-old—can slap a slice of bologna between a couple of pieces of bread.''

''I've wondered about that myself,'' Gabe admitted. ''I mean, if more people were going to be involved—if a photographer or a bunch of technicians were tagging along—I could see the need for a cook, couldn't you?''

"Of course, but that isn't the case."

"No, it isn't." He shrugged, for all appearances as bewildered by their employer's eccentric demands as Jessi, if not as worried about them. "What was Elaina's theory about all this? Assuming you discussed it with her…"

"So many times that she was beginning to get a little impatient with me." Jessi gave him a rueful smile. "You know that old saying about looking a gift horse in the mouth…? Elaina knows that by heart—and by now, so do I."

Gabe grinned. "So she thinks you should quit worrying about how easy the job sounds?"

"I believe her words were 'take the money and run.'"

"Great advice since I can't answer that question, either. Now…any other concerns?" He sat on the edge of the bench, obviously ready to spring to his feet and head to the restaurant.

"Yes, as a matter of fact," Jessi said, gently pushing his shoulder with her free hand to indicate that he might as well settle back and get comfortable again. With a soft sigh of resignation, he did just that. "I can't get a handle on August Taylor. Why do you think a man like him would have this burning need to hunt for lost treasure that may not even exist? I mean, he's already established himself as an archeologist and a writer. This just seems so…so *undignified,* not to mention a tad far-fetched."

Absently, Gabe stroked Jessi's hand, which he still held. She wondered if he'd forgotten it.

"You know that this expedition is the result of a book Taylor wrote on ghost towns, Native American myths and western folklore, don't you?"

Jessi nodded, well aware, thanks to one of Elaina's many briefings, that the archeologist-turned-journalist had already done enough research on the topics to produce a lavishly illustrated coffee-table book. "Yes, and I've wondered why the shift in focus. I mean, the chances of your really finding long lost treasure are probably slim to none."

"If not less," Gabe wryly agreed. "My own personal theory is that this impulsive quest has more to do with the poor reviews of the book and the stories in the latest tabloids than with any real desire to find gold or whatever." Now he dropped her hand, but only so he could use his hands to place his next words, like a headline, in the sky. "'Is August Taylor All Washed Up?'"

"I read that. At the time I thought it was cruel."

At once, Gabe arched an eyebrow at her as if questioning her reading tastes.

Jessi ignored him. "And now that I think about it, there was another headline, too, something about his wife, Shari, and her tennis coach."

"An affair or two have been rumored, I believe. That's a natural assumption, I expect. She's quite young—less than half his age."

"Which brings me to my third and last question—"

"Last?" He gazed longingly toward the restaurant.

"Last," Jessi replied, biting back a smile. Clearly the way to this Washingtonian's heart was through his stomach. That would be good news to a gourmet cook such as herself...if she were trying to win his heart, which she most definitely wasn't. "Is Shari's bad reputation the reason we had to get married? I mean, Elaina did make up that story about our living together for two years. Why the need for a wedding?"

"I figure one of two reasons—either Elaina's a lousy liar or our mythical cohabitation wasn't enough for him, and he wanted some hard evidence of commitment. Either way, it's clear that he doesn't trust his wife, probably the reason she's being dragged along on this expedition, and, now that I think of it, maybe even the reason you are, too. He's afraid she won't behave herself around an unattached guide as dashing as me and wants you along to keep her occupied and act as chaperon." He suddenly grinned again. "Or maybe we're all wet on this thing. Maybe *she* doesn't trust *him*, and it's the shapely cook's marital status, not the guide's, that's to blame for these mandatory nuptials—a sort of loop of suspicion.''

Jessi groaned and pressed her fingertips to her temples. "Oh please stop. You're giving me a headache.''

"The point is moot anyway.... We've tied the knot.'' For a heartbeat, he looked as if that knot might be part of a noose that now choked him. Then he gave her a half smile that could have meant anything. "You haven't said how you like the ring.''

At a loss, Jessi frowned. "What ring?''

"The one on your finger. The one I bought for you to-day.''

"Oh, of course. I'm sorry.'' For the first time, Jessi took a good look at her third finger, left hand. She saw a wide gold band as expected, but mounted on it was an exquisite, rectangular-cut amethyst. Stunned, she raised her gaze to Gabe. "I can't believe you bought this.''

"I know a diamond is traditional, but when I saw that stone and realized it matched your eyes, I had to have it.''

"My God, Gabe. We're only going to be married for a few weeks. What will you do with it after that?''

"What will you do with mine?'' he countered, raising his left hand and spreading his fingers as if to remind her of the band she'd bought for him. It looked too plain now. Embarrassingly cheap.

"It doesn't matter. It didn't cost one fourth of what this one did.'' Jessi eyed her ring, which sparkled even in the poor lighting. She'd never had anything so gorgeous—she already dreaded giving it back.

Gabe frowned, obviously picking up on her heartfelt distress. "I put it on my plastic, okay? A delayed payment plan that was part of some early Christmas promotion or something. The first charge won't even come through until February, next year. I'll return the ring long before that.''

"You think?''

"Sure, and if it doesn't work out that way...what the heck?

Call it a birthday present—I know you have one coming up shortly—'' he held up his hands to ward off her immediate protest "—or consider it payment for putting up with my shenanigans. You'll probably more than earn that ring before this is over, you know. Marriage to me—even this fake one—won't be easy.''

Jessi opened her mouth to argue but never got the chance since Gabe touched his forefinger to her lips to halt the tumbling words.

"It's done, Jessi. Can we just let it rest?''

"If that's what you really want…''

"It's what I want.''

She shrugged her shoulders in reluctant cooperation.

Visibly relieved, Gabe flashed that full-fledged, killer smile of his. "Good. Now can we please go eat the dinner Elaina graciously arranged for us? I'm so hungry, I'm weak.''

Weak, did he say?

Well, so was Jessi…but not with hunger.

It was the man who made her weak—every golden-tanned, muscled-and-toned, just-too-gorgeous inch of him. And when he reached out his hand to tug her to her feet, Jessi's heart thumped hard once, then settled into an erratic rhythm she suspected might haunt her for the duration of their brief marriage.

Chapter Two

The European-style restaurant, replica of a medieval Spanish castle, was one that Jessi had read about in a gourmet cooking magazine. She knew it had a four-star rating and that the price of even the simplest fare would set her back a week's salary, had she been footing the bill.

But she wasn't. Elaina Rivera, whom August Taylor had first contacted two weeks ago about his special employment needs, was treating tonight. Not for the first time, Jessi wished Elaina were there. Chitchat wasn't Jessi's forte.

Luckily Gabe appeared to have the gift of gab, a fact proved several times during the moments following their being seated at a table for two located in a glassed-in balcony that overlooked the city. The waiter brought champagne, complimentary for newlyweds, and a menu. Although her jittery stomach murmured mild protest at the idea of food, Jessi perused the list of the culinary delights from which she could choose.

"I'm a little out of my league here," Gabe said after a cursory glance at the elaborate menu. "Why don't you order for both of us?"

Jessi did.

Once alone with Gabe again, she raised her stemmed glass. "To our, um, lucrative partnership."

"I'll certainly drink to that." They sipped, set down their glasses and stared at one another. "Feeling better now?"

"Oh, I never felt *bad,* exactly. More nervous. I've been divorced for longer than three years now and once swore I'd never marry again unless I found the perfect man. That's the only kind that might be worth another promise of forever to my way of thinking."

Gabe winced. "I have to tell you that I'm far from perfect."

"Since forever is not in question here—wedding vows or not—that really doesn't matter," Jessi told him, adding, "I wouldn't mind hearing your faults, though. Just so I'm prepared."

Gabe nodded at the sense of that. "For starters, I can be very intense. Though tonight I may sound flippant about our expedition, the moment we join August Taylor on Monday, I'll be a different man."

"Are you saying that you actually believe there's a chance we'll find buried treasure?"

"No. I'm saying I'm being paid a hell of a lot of money to keep an open mind. Besides, I've been a tracker and guide for too many years to think I've seen it all. You just never know what's waiting around the next bend or over the next hill."

Jessi sipped her champagne while she digested his words. "So you're dedicated to duty, huh? Well, I've just enough experience with men who *aren't*—my ex-husband, to name one—to consider that a plus instead of a minus. What are your other so-called character flaws?"

"I'm a grump before my morning coffee. I'm a slob around the house. I talk too much and listen too little...or so *my* ex always told me."

"You're divorced? Somehow I missed that little detail."

"That's because it wasn't on my fact sheet. I didn't think

it would make any difference to anyone. I've been single ten years now.''

"Any children?''

"No, thank goodness.''

Jessi frowned. "You don't like them?'' August Taylor had graciously agreed to let Anna Kate go along on the expedition, probably because it would be little more than an extended camping trip for the women. If Gabe didn't like children, their "home life'' might be less than ideal and a source of stress for Jessi's daughter.

"I love kids, and I think they're the innocent victims of any divorce. I'm personally glad I didn't father any because my ex-wife would almost certainly have gotten custody, thanks to my gypsy lifestyle at the time and in the ten years since. All that's going to change now, of course.''

"In what way?''

"Elaina didn't share my motives for agreeing to this expedition?''

"Actually, I never asked. I assumed you must have creditors breathing down your neck, just as I do.''

"No past expenditures, just future ones. First, the purchase of some acres on the Snake River in Washington. They now belong to a friend named Jerry Clark who has a canoe rental, café and sporting goods store on them. When he told me he was ready to retire, I scraped together enough earnest money for him to hold the land. What I get from August plus a loan from the bank will cinch the deal and put me in business. As for the second expenditure, well, it's of a whole different nature so I can't really predict how much money I'll need. God only knows what it costs to adopt and raise a kid these days.''

"You're going to adopt a child?''

"I'm going to try. He's my nephew. Son of my adopted sister, who was shot during a convenience store robbery three months ago in L.A.''

"Oh, Gabe, I'm so sorry,'' Jessi murmured, noting how a flush stained his cheeks and how his eyes brimmed.

Clearly this was a wound that had not healed. "How old is the boy?"

"Ten."

"And where is he now?"

"In foster care. Kids his age aren't in high demand adoption-wise. Most folks want babies."

"And his father?"

"Long gone just like my real one." Gabe gave Jessi a wry smile. "All I know about my mother is that she gave me up when I was born because my father wouldn't marry her. I was one of two kids adopted by a military man and his wife. He died when I was ten and Geena, er, my adopted sister, was four. My new mom, who apparently hadn't wanted to adopt children in the first place, remarried six months later and pretty much ignored Geena and me. I hated the guy and wanted to leave then, but I couldn't afford it, of course, until I turned eighteen, when I got a job as dispatcher for a rescue team in the Cascades. One of the guys proved to be a strong father figure. He really put me on the right track."

"Jerry Clark?"

Gabe nodded and smiled. "You're very quick. I'd better remember that." He turned the glass around and around in his fingers. "I just wish there'd been a role model around for Geena. Unfortunately, there wasn't, so when she turned sixteen, she ran off with some guy who promised her the moon, but gave her nothing more than a hard time and a son. She finally found the guts to leave him, but her life went downhill from there.

"I sent her money when I could," he continued. "She wouldn't let me help any other way." His voice sounded oddly bereft of emotion at this point, almost as if he were numb on the subject. "But no one is going to stop me from making a home for her son Ryder as soon as possible. Meanwhile I have to be content with a weekly phone call and one visit per month since he's still in L.A., which is too far away from my place in Washington for anything more.''

''You think a judge will give you custody?''

Gabe's eyes flashed, revealing the stubborn side she had heretofore only suspected. ''I'm all the family that kid has, I'm willing, and soon I'll be settled down with a viable business. Why the hell wouldn't I get custody?''

Jessi could think of several reasons right away, not the least of which would be their own annulment. She said nothing, however.

Gabe smirked just a little when she didn't speak, obviously assuming he'd made his point. ''Now that we've settled that, I believe it's your turn to confess, Jessi Dillard.''

Startled by his use of her new name—a cold reminder that this wasn't just dinner with an interesting stranger—Jessi could only stammer, ''I—I don't have anything to confess.''

At that moment, the waiter walked up with a tray of hors d'oeuvres. Grateful for the diversion, Jessi selected for both of them again and then thanked the man, who left them alone again too soon.

''These, um, look scrumptious,'' she murmured. ''Try one.''

Gabe glanced from Jessi to the appetizer she offered, then back to Jessi again. He arched an eyebrow at her. ''As my wife, you stand to inherit if I die of food poisoning, don't you?''

Jessi actually laughed and marveled that she could respond so easily to his teasing in her present state of nervousness. Clearly what she still didn't know about this man's character might fill the pages of a book, yet the one trait she was sure of, his sense of humor, almost put her at ease.

Almost.

''Shall I be the royal taster?'' With a hand that still wasn't steady, Jessi picked up one of the artful delicacies and took a bite, savoring the pungent spices.

"Good?" Gabe asked.

"Divine."

"I'm a meat and potatoes man myself."

"Are you telling me that's all I'm going to be able to cook on this trip?"

"August Taylor is your boss, not me. I expect he and his missus are used to fancy fare."

"It's actually remarkably easy to get used to." Jessi reached over to pick up one of Gabe's hors d'oeuvres. She raised it to his mouth, which he dutifully opened. Slowly, looking as if he might be sampling baked rattlesnake, Gabe chewed.

Almost instantly, his powder-blue eyes lit up. "This is excellent."

"You thought I'd lie to you?"

"That could be one of the character flaws you don't need to confess."

"It could be, but it isn't," Jessi retorted, the next moment belatedly registering the enormity of tonight's transgression. At once the doubts stuffed in the back of her mind the past week exploded to the forefront with a vengeance, leaving her anxious and confused. "Or maybe I should say it *wasn't*." She frowned and pushed her plate away, having suddenly lost all desire to eat. "God, I hate lying. And I can't believe that I let greed get the best of my scruples. Normally, I'm honest to a fault."

"You're only human, and greed is a very human emotion. Why, I'll bet the problems of ninety-nine percent of the men and women who populate the prisons of this nation are rooted in that. Unfortunately, they got caught in the process of satisfying it."

"And what happens if we get caught?"

Gabe sat in silence, his dark brows knitted in a frown. "August Taylor tosses us into a rattlesnake pit and rolls a stone across the entrance?"

"This isn't funny, it's wrong…very wrong. We're part of a scam. We're deceiving this man for his money."

"Lighten up. All we've done is pretend we were lovers before we married. That's an insignificant deceit when you consider that he's going to have the best damn guide in the country, not to mention a gourmet cook, at his beck and call for however long it takes."

Jessi shrugged away the rationalization. "A lie is a lie is a lie."

"What are you saying?"

"I'm saying I've felt awful about this whole marriage thing all day, and at this moment I don't think I can go through with it."

Gabe's jaw dropped. "You can't be serious."

"As war." Jessi hesitated only a second longer before doing what she knew in her heart of hearts had to be done: tugging off the ring and handing it to him.

"Just a damn minute!" Gabe caught her wrist with his free hand and stared at her in total disbelief, clearly as astonished as Jessi that she could change her mind at this late date. "Have you forgotten how much money is at stake here?"

"How could I? That's what got me into this mess in the first place." Jessi shook her head, honestly regretful to be throwing a monkey wrench into his big plans, but knowing she had no choice. "I'm so sorry. I thought I could do this…I mean I *really* did. But how can I possibly face that man day in and day out, knowing that I've lied about something that matters so much to him—"

"For God's sake, would you just listen—"

She held up her free hand to halt his words. "No, Gabe. It's no use arguing. I can't go through with it, and that's that."

"That is *not* that, Jessi. My future with Ryder hangs in the balance here. You can't possibly back out now."

"You're wrong. Now is exactly the time to do this—before things go one step further." She sagged under the weight of his stare. "Look…I'm really sorry about Ryder, but I believe you'll find a way to get him and maybe even

that land you want. As for Elaina...I'll talk to her myself.
I'll take full responsibility for everything.''

Gabe abruptly released her wrist and sat back in his
chair, his expression now cool. ''Fine, then. Do what you
must. But you might want to get yourself a good lawyer
before you make any calls to Elaina.''

''Why would I need a lawyer? Technically, our marriage
license isn't legal until it's filed.''

''The license may not be, but Elaina's agency contract
sure as hell is.''

''That was just a formality,'' Jessi replied, waving away
his foolish concerns. ''All it said was that she'd get a per-
centage of whatever salary I earned, which would only be
fair.''

''Did you read the small print?''

Jessi bristled. ''I read the whole thing.''

''Then you recall that you promised to pay that percent-
age whether or not you held up your end of the employment
bargain.''

''No....''

''Oh yes. I believe that particular clause was in the middle of the thing, surrounded by several whereas-es and
wherefores.''

Slowly Jessi raised her gaze to Gabe, who grimaced an
apology, though the fault was clearly her own. ''I don't
have that kind of money.''

''Neither do I, so why don't we just go on as planned?
In time you'll get used to the lie.''

''Never.''

He digested that, his face solemn and thoughtful.
''Maybe if we found an alternative solution to your moral
dilemma...''

''There is one?''

''Yes. Admittedly it is a bit radical given the length of
our acquaintance, but no more than this marriage of ours.
And, thanks to that marriage, it would be both morally and
legally acceptable.''

Jessi frowned, a little leery of his double talk. "Just what does this solution entail?"

"Consummation."

"Excuse me?"

"Sex. You and me. Tonight. So what if we have our sequence of events a little reversed? At least we'll be experienced lovers when we look ol' August in the eye Monday. That beats the heck out of inexperienced liars, don't you think?"

"Get real." The nerve of the man to think she'd sleep with the likes of him! Never mind her earlier admiration for his good looks. He did not light her fire. And the only reason she now grabbed her wine glass and gulped down the chilled liquid was to keep from punching him out.

"I take it that's a no."

Jessi glared at him over the rim of her glass. "That's a 'don't even think about it.'"

He accepted rejection with an easy shrug. "I'd be less than normal if I never thought about it. You are one classy lady—the kind that gets a man's attention and keeps it."

"I can't believe you're saying this to me. Why, it's sexual harassment, that's what it is."

"We're married, for crying out loud!"

"In name only, remember? As far as I'm concerned, this is a business partnership, nothing more. I don't want to hear about your fantasies."

"Hmm, well, I'd love to hear about yours...but I won't press for details beyond asking what it is about me that makes my solution to your dilemma unacceptable."

Jessi's jaw dropped. "I don't love you."

Gabe considered that. "So you're an old-fashioned girl, huh?"

"You're damn right, mister...only I prefer to call it traditional. Sex is not something I take lightly. And I'd never sleep with some man just because I found him attractive."

"Are you saying you find me attractive?"

Well hell. "N-no."

"Then you're saying you don't find me attractive."

"No."

He huffed his impatience. "Do you or do you not find me the least bit attractive?"

"What an ego!" Jessi exclaimed, slapping her hand down on the table. "What difference does it make when I already told you I have no intentions of consummating this fictional marriage?"

"I just like to know where I stand, that's all. Is that too much to ask?"

"Frankly, yes."

"Oh, come on, Jessi. You said you're always honest. Be honest with me now. Is there anything that you like about me...anything at all?"

Jessi, who could easily think of thousands of things, fumbled for an answer that wouldn't further encourage this pointless, embarrassing conversation. "You have a nice smile."

"That's all?"

"And pretty blue eyes."

"Nothing else?"

"You love your nephew."

He sighed. "Well, that's a start, I guess."

A start? "No, that's the finish. Now I don't want to hear another word about this, okay? Work relations will be strained, if not impossible, if you're constantly coming on to me."

"Work relations? Does that mean you've changed your mind about wanting to back out?"

"No. I still want to back out. As I now see it, however, I really have no choice but to go through with this thing. If I don't, I'll not only have to find a way to pay my creditors, I'll have to find a way to pay Elaina, too." She sighed. "The fact is, I need August Taylor's money, and I need it bad."

"So do I, and speaking of which...you do realize you're

going to have to waste some of your hard-earned cash on
an annulment…?''

Jessi frowned. ''Actually, I figured we'd split the costs
of that.''

''And so we will, if there are any.''

''What do you mean 'if there are any'? No legal pro-
ceeding is cheap, Gabe.'' She gave him a hopeful smile.
''Unless you have a lawyer friend…?''

''No lawyer friend, just an idea.''

''Oh no,'' Jessi groaned. *''Another one?''*

Gabe glared at her, clearly affronted.

''Sorry,'' she murmured, instantly contrite. ''What's
your idea?''

''We forget about filing the license on Monday. If there's
no legal marriage, then there's no need for an annulment.''

Jessi caught her breath at the simplicity, the sheer *per-
fection* of his idea. ''And if there's not another split on your
record, then your chances of getting Ryder are that much
better.…'' She spoke to herself more than to Gabe, so the
impact of her words caught her by surprise.

''My God.…'' Her new husband paled and stared at her,
his eyes huge with shock. ''Would you believe this is the
first time I'd even thought about how our break up might
affect the adoption proceedings?''

''But if we never file, there will be no annulment because
in the eyes of the law, there has been no marriage.'' They
exchanged a long, speculative look during which neither
said a word. Then Gabe held out his left hand, palm upward. In it lay the ring.

Jessi stared at it for a moment without moving. To accept
the ring meant she accepted the terms of their partnership,
and the deceit that went with it, once and for all. *What do
I do…what do I do…?*

''Please? For Ryder's sake?'' The words were whisper-
soft and shimmied down her spine.

Jessi sucked in a fortifying breath and reached for the
ring, only to find her wrist captured in his right hand again.

With a smile that could only be called tender, he slipped the bejeweled band back on her finger.

The amethyst caught the light and flashed a rainbow on the wine glass. The colors were as brilliant and bold as ever, blinding her to consequences once again.

Chapter Three

Gabe Dillard couldn't remember when he'd seen a more colorful autumn. The brilliantly golden aspen trees lining the dirt path down which he now drove contrasted sharply to a gray California sky. God, how he wished Ryder were along to share the joy.

Gabe shifted his gaze from the asphalt to Jessi's petite daughter, Anna Kate, who sat between the two of them on the seat of his four-wheel drive truck. He took note of the child's attire—faded denim overalls, bright purple T-shirt, polka-dotted sneakers—and smiled to himself. With her mother's violet eyes and a riotous mass of long, copper-colored hair, Anna Kate appeared custom made for eyelet and patent leather. Oddly enough, she'd proved to be a tomboy to the nth degree, a fact discovered Sunday, when they spent the day together to get to know one another.

Anna Kate had accepted him easily, thank God, and called him "Daddy G"—a name of her creation. But in spite of their smooth sailing so far, he half wished the red-haired charmer hadn't come along on the trip. Children were so very honest. She could easily jeopardize their cha-rade.

But Jessi had sworn that Anna Kate was special, a natural actress who adored pretending. It helped that the child had apparently begged for a new daddy for ages. And though Jessi had made it plain to her daughter that Gabe was noth-ing more than a daddy-on-loan who would one day be gone again, he couldn't help but wonder about the impact their parting a few weeks from now would have on her.

Other things bothered him, too, not the least of which was involving an innocent child in their deception. But what else could he do except come clean with August, a risk he wasn't prepared or willing to take? As he'd told Jessi, their lie was a harmless one necessitated by August's apparent midlife crisis and, perhaps, his autocratic ways. The flamboyant archeologist and author had been in the limelight for twenty-five years, so he was used to people hopping when he snapped "Frog!" Only in the past twelve months had his popularity begun to slide, the reason, Gabe believed, for this desperate, top-secret, possibly ridiculous expedition.

A splash of bright blue paint on the side of a tree in a valley below alerted Gabe that he'd almost reached the turnoff leading to the location of their three o'clock ren-dezvous with Taylor. He caught a glimpse of the two camper trailers he'd rented, along with the boxes filled full of everything else that could possibly be needed for an expedition of this type.

August had been camped at the site since the day before. He and Gabe had been in constant contact via the man's cellular phone, just one of the modern-day miracles that made it possible to conduct business from anywhere. There were other conveniences, too, including bathrooms, all-terrain vehicles that would save them miles of walking, a stove so they could cook indoors in the wildest of woods and even a battery-powered television. They also had a pro-pane-fueled refrigerator.

So much for roughing it, Gabe thought, glancing beyond the valley to the colorful cliffs of the Sierra Nevada mountain range. Was there treasure in *them thar hills?* In his heart of hearts, he didn't think so. But if, by some strange chance, there were, he'd find it. He was a damn good explorer who'd made a name for himself in this state years ago, the reason Elaina was told about him when she contacted the California Game and Fish Agency for a top-notch guide to lead this treasure hunt. Gabe didn't know how she'd found Jessi, but her choice of chief cook and bottle washer suited him.

Yeah...suited him just fine.

The ground dipped sharply and so did the truck, nearly jerking the steering wheel out of Gabe's hand. Then the vehicle lurched to the right, badly jarring its occupants.

"You okay?" Gabe asked Anna Kate.

She nodded, looking for all the world as if bumpy truck rides and treasure hunts were everyday occurrences for her. Bemused, Gabe stole a glance at Anna Kate's mother, who peered out her window and into the woods.

Jessi didn't look nearly so at ease, a sure sign she still had doubts about her well-paid position of cook and glorified baby-sitter for August Taylor's pampered wife. On top of that, Gabe guessed this whole great outdoors thing must be somewhat stressful for her. She was, by vocation, a woman used to the more genteel things in life—catered luncheons, afternoon teas, formal banquets. She appeared uncomfortable in the sweater, jeans and tennis shoes she wore. But even dressed in such, there was no doubt of her good breeding.

He hadn't lied Saturday night when predicting he'd probably wish again for a consummation of their wedding vows. The woman had fascinated him from the moment they met. Just the thought of kissing her, touching her set him on fire, the reason he'd opted for a handshake at the wedding. A kiss at that point or any other would be disaster—a shock to his libido—that would surely have resulted in a shift of his attention from one kind of treasure to another, namely Jessi.

Thank God, she'd rejected that foolish, impromptu Plan A. Gabe knew without a doubt that if Jessi had welcomed him into her bed Saturday night, they'd still be there today. She was that kind of woman. And a man with as many plans as Gabe just didn't have time for the distraction.

"Who's that?" Anna Kate asked, a question that brought Gabe back to the here and now.

Slowing the truck, waving to the man in question, Gabe nodded. "That's Mr. Taylor, our boss. Looks like a big ol' bear, doesn't he?"

Anna Kate giggled. Jessi groaned, no doubt wanting to throttle Gabe for encouraging his stepdaughter's imagination. But to Gabe's way of thinking, August did have some physical characteristics a child might connect with a forest-dwelling creature.

Tall—a good half foot over six feet—with a shock of raven hair and a full, gray-streaked beard, the man was unforgettable to say the least. Dressed as he was today in camouflage from his Aussie-styled hat to custom-made hiking boots, August blended in beautifully with the woods. Next to him was his wife, Shari. A former model, she stood tall enough to be a perfect physical mate for August.

The truck lurched to a halt at the edge of the clearing where the man and woman worked. August immediately strode over to them, waiting until Gabe killed the engine and stepped out of the vehicle, then thrust out his right hand.

"How was your trip?"

"Great," Gabe said, trying not to groan with pain from August's bone-crushing handshake. He ducked to look back in the car.

"Out, ladies. I want you to meet the boss."

Anna Kate tossed off her safety belt, scrambled across the leather seat and stood on the driver's side, arms outstretched to Gabe. He assisted her to the ground via an overhead swing that made her squeal and laugh. By the time he set Anna Kate on her feet, all smiles and blush, Jessi had joined them.

Introductions were quick and casual. Since Jessi didn't wince when August shook her hand, Gabe could only assume the man had a gentler touch where the fairer sex was concerned.

And Jessi, with her peachy skin and auburn hair, was certainly that.

At that moment, Shari joined them. Although tagged as a witch with a capital *W* by the tabloids and scoop television, she smiled with delight at Anna Kate, who smiled right back and struck up a conversation about her ash blond hair.

Watching how easily Shari related to Anna Kate and then to Jessi, Gabe guessed the woman had gotten a bum rap from the media as had so many other celebrities in the past. No doubt jealousy was the motive. She was a beauty—statuesque, shapely, striking.

Most men's fantasy.

Not his, however. Statuesque equated to too tall; shapely, to too thin; and striking, to too perfect. He preferred women who were shorter and fuller, like Jessi, who was nonetheless petite. As for Shari's beauty...while he couldn't deny her classic good looks, he found himself thinking that a light sprinkling of freckles across her nose would do wonders for her face.

Just look what they did for Jessi's.

"We need to talk privately before you brief us on travel plans and daily routine," August said.

"Sure." Gabe followed his boss to his camper trailer. Larger of necessity than the RV Gabe and Jessi would inhabit, it boasted office space furnished to August's specific needs. There was also a small darkroom for developing any photographs they might take. August, of course, intended to man the camera himself, and when he wanted to be in the shot, Gabe would. Since no one else was going on the search except the two women and Anna Kate, Gabe suspected each of them soon would discover hidden talents of their own.

When they stepped into the trailer, August motioned for Gabe to sit. Gabe chose the tiny couch and settled in, waiting to hear whatever August had to say. He wasn't worried. So far, he and his boss seemed to be on the same wavelength, and he'd done everything required of him and more when planning this expedition.

"Shari thinks I owe you an apology."

Gabe arched an eyebrow. "Oh yeah?"

August nodded and looked away. "She wasn't very happy with me when she found out I insisted that you and Jessi get married. She told me I should mind my own business."

"I see."

"I guess I'm telling you this a little late. Elaina did fax the license Saturday night."

"So she said."

"I don't want us to get started on the wrong foot. Normally, I'm not so...persistent or interfering. I, um, just thought it would be better for all concerned. Privacy will be minimal at times...but that wouldn't have mattered, would it? You two have been living together for...how long?"

Gabe went blank. "Long enough to know Jessi's the one for me," he blurted, adding, "Don't worry about the wedding. You just expedited the inevitable and probably did us both a big favor. It's a commitment we might never have gotten around to."

"I doubt that. Any fool could see that you two are devoted to each other. And if I'd met her earlier, I'd never have demanded a wedding."

At once, Gabe wondered if now might not be the perfect time to tell August the truth. It seemed that the man might accept it. They could rent another motor home for Jessi and Anna Kate. Everyone would be happy...except, he abruptly realized, himself. Now that he'd gotten used to the idea of sharing a roof with Jessi and her daughter, he wasn't particularly eager to let go of it. All that was missing was Ryder, who'd complete the picture of a perfect family.

"You just seemed a bit too footloose when we first talked," August continued. "On the prowl, if you will."

That's because I was, Gabe thought.

"And I was worried that…well—" Abruptly, he ended the sentence with a shrug of apology, leaving Gabe to guess at his meaning.

"There's nothing to worry about now. We're good and married." And would stay that way—at least for a while— since Gabe had no intentions of sharing the details of this little tête-à-tête with his new wife.

August nodded and stood, no doubt indicating an end to their talk. Gabe did the same and moved toward the door, where, on impulse, he paused and looked back.

"I probably shouldn't say this.…" Gabe hesitated, suddenly consumed by second thoughts about the wisdom of advising this man, or any other, on his love life. God knows, he was in no position.

"I prefer honesty."

"I think you worry too much. Your wife seems very nice and very much in love with you." August said nothing, and Gabe guessed he'd overstepped his bounds. Muttering "I'll get the women together for our meeting," Gabe quickly left the trailer.

A glance around the clearing revealed that Jessi, Anna Kate, and Shari were coming out of the trailer that would be the Dillard home for a while. Gabe perused Jessi's expression, trying to decide how she felt about the place. She looked pleased, he thought, a sure indication that the three-room house on wheels would do. As for Anna Kate, she leapt from the bottom step to the dirt, landing flat-footed, then dashed to the Taylors' motor home and entered it uninvited.

Clearly flustered, Jessi started after her, but stopped when

Gabe waved her away. August might as well get used to having the kid around. Short of tying Anna Kate to a tree, Jessi wouldn't be able to contain her daughter's natural curiosity and four-year-old energy without making everyone miserable.

Almost immediately, August came out of the trailer, Anna Kate in his arms. She rubbed his bushy beard and laughed. Gabe could've sworn he saw a smile tugging at the corners of the man's mouth and noted that Shari's jaw dropped at the sight, leaving him to wonder if the couple knew each other at all. Clearly, Shari hadn't expected August to like Anna Kate, though it was at her insistence, at least according to Elaina, that she was allowed to come along. Was there a hidden agenda? Life—or marriage—lessons to be learned?

Probably, Gabe decided, and August might not be the only student. These next weeks playing husband to Jessi and daddy to Anna Kate would undoubtedly be a learning experience for him, too—preparation for Ryder. And his impulsive decision to maintain his and Jessi's deceit would be one he surely rued when all was said and done.

"Everyone ready to be briefed?" Gabe asked to get the attention of his companions.

Immediately, they gravitated in his direction and sat wherever they could—Gabe on the lowered tailgate of his truck, now accessible since the hatchback of the camper top had been raised; Anna Kate on a stump, and Shari and Jessi sharing a fallen log. August chose to lean against a tall pine tree.

"As you probably know, we're going to cover a lot of ground in the next three to four weeks. August, here, has done his homework the past several months, researching countless north and southwest lost treasure legends. Based on the information he's gathered, I've mapped out our expedition, and I can tell you that we've got ten locations to explore in a very short time, so we've got our work cut out for us."

Jessi and Shari exchanged a glance at that point, making Gabe wonder what they'd been talking about since they met. Belatedly, it occurred to him that Shari could have told Jessi that she'd scolded her husband for demanding a wedding. If so, Jessi might have spilled the truth—women were notorious for that in his opinion—a disconcerting possibility he'd somehow have to confirm or disprove without showing his own hand. How else would he know where he stood?

"Do these locations have names?" Jessi asked.

Gabe realized he had better concentrate on the matter at hand instead of worrying about what she might or might not know.

"Actually, most of them are nothing more than dots on a map, if that," Gabe replied. "And most are in the middle of nowhere, just like this."

"Will there be any dangerous wildlife to worry about?" Jessi stole a glance at her daughter, almost as if having second—or was it fourth by now?—thoughts.

"I'll answer that one, Gabe," August interjected as though reading those thoughts. "There's always a risk of encountering wildlife, and some of it could be dangerous. Campsites have been carefully selected with safety in mind, however. I wouldn't risk any of you ladies."

"Any reason why we're starting this treasure hunt here in these mountains?" Shari asked, confirming Gabe's suspicion that she was just along for the ride and knew little about the actual game plan.

"Yes. My most promising lead comes from the journal of a gold miner, one Silas McHenry. His great-grandniece let me reprint passages of it for my book. I have one here I'd like to share." August took a piece of paper out of his shirt pocket, unfolded it and read:

"'November 13, 1849. John thinks someone is watching us from the mountains, waiting for the right moment to take advantage of our good luck. He won't even close his eyes at night for fear we'll be murdered in our beds. I told him that cave we found up on Panther Ridge would make a good hiding place for our treasures.'"

"Treasure*s*?" Shari asked. "Plural?"

"That's right," August answered with a nod.

"Odd way to put it," Jessi murmured.

Her expressive eyes, window to her thoughts, sparkled with speculation and curiosity. Gabe grinned, glad to note that her reservations about this little trip had apparently been forgotten…at least for the moment.

"Not if the men, who were certainly partners, split whatever gold they found each day." August bent down and picked up a rock, examined it, then gave it a toss into the trees. "Silas McHenry, according to his great-grandniece and only living descendant, was a young journalist from Philadelphia. When he heard about the California gold rush, he decided to try his luck and filled up the pages of several journals in the process. Unfortunately, that luck ran out in these very mountains when whoever was watching him and his partner apparently decided to attack…or that's the theory. No one knows exactly what happened, of course, but apparently all that was ever found of the two miners were these journals."

"I can't believe no one's tried to find their gold before now," Shari murmured. "Especially since you reprinted this in your book."

"Who says they haven't?" August retorted.

"You mean there've been other searches for this cave?"

"Lots, I expect," August said with a nod. "At least two big ones that were documented, and both ended in disaster."

Jessi frowned. "Exactly what kind of disaster?"

August hesitated a heartbeat before answering. "The men looking for the treasure never returned from the mountains."

"You're kidding, right?" Shari's eyes were round as cupcakes.

August just shook his head. "Don't you remember in my book?"

Shari thought for a moment, then her jaw dropped. "Oh, God...the one called 'The McHenry Curse'?"

"Yes, but there's nothing to worry about," August said. "If anything really happened to those other treasure hunters it's because of bad planning and not any curse. I've hired the best guide in the country, and he's got the situation well in hand." August nodded to Gabe. "And on that note, I think I'll turn the floor—er, ground—back over to him."

Great, Gabe thought, highly aware of the accusing stares of the two women, now focused on him. "Thanks, boss. There are, um, just the four of us—well, five, counting Miss Priss, here." Gabe managed a grin for Anna Kate, who promptly stuck out her tongue at him and lightened the moment for everyone. "Obviously we're each going to have to be Jacks-and-Jills-of-all-trades. Besides guiding, I'll be in charge of maintaining supplies, keeping the vehicles fueled, and first aid, plus whatever else needs to be done to keep August free to do his thing. Jessi is in charge of cooking. Shari, I understand you're going to act as August's secretary...?" Somehow he couldn't picture her at a keyboard, typing up her husband's notes.

"B.A. in Business, UCLA," she replied, as if on cue. She grinned, clearly enjoying the shock that must be as evident on his face as it was on Jessi's. "I was *discovered*—" she drew quotation marks in the air with the first two fingers of both hands "—in a beauty pageant, my last year there."

"Really?" Jessi murmured.

"Really," Shari confirmed, adding, "And I'm going to do more than just type August's notes. I intend to help Jessi around camp."

"You don't have to do that," Jessi hastily interjected.

"Oh, I don't mind. It'll be fun—probably because I

never get to do much at home. We have a live-in house-keeper.'' She shot an accusing glance at her husband, who looked away.

Gabe wondered if they did not always agree on her role in the marriage.

Gabe noted Jessi's thoughtful expression and wondered if she were thinking what he was thinking—clearly all was not well between Shari and August, exactly as Gabe and Jessi had already decided. But he wasn't being paid to wonder about his boss's personal life, just to do his bidding.

''What about me?'' Anna Kate piped up just then. ''What's my job?''

''To keep us smiling,'' Gabe told her, reaching over to tweak her uptilted nose.

Anna Kate pushed his hand away and pouted. ''But I wanna really help.''

''You can be in charge of gathering wood for the camp-fire,'' August told her.

The child's eyes rounded with delight. ''We're gonna have a campfire?''

''Bingo! *If* you do your job.''

''Oh, I will. I will.'' She hopped off her perch. ''I'll find the biggest, bestest wood ever…starting now!''

''Whoa!'' Gabe exclaimed, capturing her by the sus-penders. ''There's a rule you have to memorize before you start wandering. A rule everyone has to memorize.'' He looked at each of the females in turn, ascertaining that he had their undivided attention. ''Never go out of sight of the trailers unless I'm along. Never. We're going to be camping in some pretty wild country. I don't want to end up hunting for you instead of the treasure.'' He focused his gaze on Anna Kate. ''Now raise your left hand—no, honey, the other one—and repeat after me—I will never, ever leave camp without telling someone…''

Anna Kate rocked back on her heels and recited the words, solemn as he'd ever seen her or probably ever would again. "'I will never, ever leave camp without telling some-one…'"

Gabe nodded approval. "And I'll never go so far that I can't see the trailers."

"'And I'll never'… 'I'll never'… I forgot…"

"Go so far that I can't see the trailers."

"Go so I can't see the trailers."

"That'll do." He ruffled her curls, which felt silky soft to his work-roughened hand. "As for daily routine, I really can't predict that beyond saying three meals a day would be nice, but may not always be necessary as August and I will most likely be away from camp during the day." He scanned the faces of his audience. "Any questions?" Everyone shook their heads. "Well, that's it I guess." He turned to Anna Kate. "Why don't I go with you to collect wood this first time so you'll know what kind burns best?"

"I can do it myself."

"Yeah, well there's a cliff to the east and I don't want you falling off it."

Anna Kate rolled her eyes and sighed. "Okay, Daddy G," she murmured, holding out her hand to him. Together, they walked into the trees immediately surrounding the clearing, where they began to search the leaf-strewn forest floor for fallen limbs.

"Cute kid," Shari murmured to Jessi. "Wish I had one."

"That should be easy enough to arrange," Jessi teased, glancing at August, who ambled back to his motor home.

"Not as easy as you'd think." Shari gave her a wan smile. "He thinks he's too old."

"That's ridiculous."

"So I've told him. He doesn't believe me. That's the reason I pressed him to let your daughter come along, of course. I thought she'd be good for him. I hope you don't mind the ulterior motive."

"I'm just glad he agreed."

There was a moment's silence, then Shari stood. "Guess

we'd better get started unloading those boxes. It'll be dark soon."

"I really don't expect you to help," Jessi said, standing. "I'm sure you have more important things to do."

"Like what? Do my nails?" Shari shook her head. "I realize you're being paid to cook and baby-sit me—" she smiled, clearly picking up on Jessi's surprise at that blunt interpretation of their situation "—but I was really hoping we could be friends."

"I'd like that a lot," Jessi said, and meant it.

"Then let me do what any friend would do—help you. And in return, you can help me."

"I'm afraid I'm not much of a typist."

Shari laughed. "Oh, I didn't mean that. I want to learn to cook something besides scrambled eggs and toast, which is my one and only specialty. Would you teach me?"

"Gladly," Jessi told her, impulsively adding a hug to seal the bargain. When she released the slender beauty, she discovered that Shari's eyes brimmed with tears. Dismayed, Jessi blurted, "What's wrong?"

"Everything, but it's going to get better. I just know it." She glanced off into the woods, where Gabe and Anna Kate still walked, arms now loaded with logs. "You're so lucky, Jessi."

Jessi followed her gaze and noted how very natural Anna Kate and Gabe looked together. She realized with a start that she must indeed seem lucky. Handsome husband. Darling daughter. From all appearances, she had it all.

But appearances could be deceiving, the reason her gut knotted with something very akin to regret. No handsome husband...at least not in the forever sense. She closed her eyes, for just a second letting her mind wander at will. Not surprisingly, visions of Gabe filled her head. She saw the twinkle in his eyes, those dashing dimples, that sexy smile. And there was more to her fantasy, more of him than that—characteristics, in truth, unseen; characteristics that her imagination supplied with shocking ease.

"Jessi?"

Broad bare shoulders and powerful arms. Great pecs. Narrow waist. Nicely rounded hips and muscled thighs. Her arms ached to pull him close. Her fingers itched to explore. She imagined herself in the double bed in their RV, felt the mattress dip as Gabe slipped between cool cotton sheets to stretch out beside her.

Had she ever felt such pure sexual excitement before? Jessi knew she hadn't. Les, her ex-husband, was a selfish lover. It hadn't helped that she'd been inexperienced in such matters. She knew the score now, however—knew that she had a right to receive as much pleasure as she gave.

"Oh, Jes-si...."

Gabe, she suspected, would be good in bed. A thoughtful lover who'd make sex the thrill it should be. Too bad she'd never get the chance to see if their reality could live up to her fantasy.

"Earth to Jessi! Please come in."

With a start, Jessi realized that a laughing Shari was trying to get her attention.

"Oh, gosh, I'm sorry. I was a million miles away."

"A million miles," Shari teased. "Or—" she glanced at Gabe—"twenty yards?"

Blushing, flustered, Jessi dared not reply.

"It's a shame you two didn't have time for a honeymoon," the blonde then murmured as if reading her companion's X-rated thoughts. "There won't be any privacy in that RV of yours."

"Oh, that's okay," Jessi quickly replied. "We don't need privacy. We've been together for, um, years now. The newness has worn off."

"I don't believe it."

Jessi's heart stopped. "Excuse me?"

"I don't believe the newness has worn off. Why, the looks that man gives you could melt steel." She smiled. "And one of these nights in the not-so-distant future, I'm going to invite Anna Kate to a sleepover that will give the two of you the privacy you deserve.''

"Oh please don't,'' Jessi blurted, horrified at the thought of such temptation. "I mean, Anna Kate can be such a handful.''

"We'll have a great time,'' Shari assured her, smiling wickedly when she added, "And so, I'll bet, will the two of you.''

Chapter Four

It wasn't easy to put Shari's prediction out of her head, but Jessi did exactly that for the rest of that Monday by focusing on her new job as cook. She chose to prepare her first meal on the stove inside the spacious RV she would call home for a while, even though there were other cooking choices, namely an open campfire and a portable barbecue rig. Jessi served dinner indoors that night, too, instead of in the camp dining room, which was really just a centrally located tent with netting sides to keep out insects.

Her hearty tomato-and-beef stew was a big hit with everyone, in particular the men, who helped themselves to seconds and then thirds, complimenting her with every bowl. After the meal, the five of them went outside and, since it was a beautiful night, sat around a campfire that resulted from Anna Kate's meticulous wood gathering.

The child sat as close to Gabe as she could sit while they all relaxed and talked, but he didn't seem to mind. Jessi herself sat clear across the campfire from the two of them, with August and Shari to her immediate left. She relished the absence of city noises and marveled at how many other sounds—foreign sounds—filled the air around them.

The buzzes, of course, could be credited to insects, Jessi decided, and the chirps to birds that hadn't turned in for the night. The tree frogs and cicadas she recognized, too, but what was that weird-sounding yowl? A cat of some kind? A wolf?

Suddenly a little spooked—a feeling not alleviated when she realized Gabe actually had a hunting rifle within reach—Jessi wondered if Anna Kate were frightened by the wild sounds. The child was so young and had never been out of the city. At that moment Anna Kate crawled right into Gabe's lap, a certain indication she might be a little nervous about their wilderness surroundings, too.

"Tell me a real scary story, Daddy G," she demanded, grabbing a handful of his shirt and pulling him down so that the tip of his nose was barely an inch from hers.

Jessi wanted to laugh. So much for fear in the under-five set.

Gabe considered her request for a moment, his questioning gaze on Jessi, who shook her head slightly to discourage him. "Will you settle for a tall tale instead?" he finally asked, gently disentangling his shirt from Anna Kate's grip.

The child nodded eagerly.

"Okay." Gabe sat in silence for another half second, then nodded to himself as if he'd made a mental selection. "Actually," he began, "the story I'm about to tell you is said to be true. Maybe it is, maybe not. I really don't know, so we'll call it a tall tale."

Jessi glanced around, noting with amusement that August and Shari looked as intrigued as Anna Kate. Relaxing, Jessi settled back against a tree, crossed her arms over her chest and waited for Gabe's story.

"This tale is about Davy Crockett," he began. "Have you heard of him?"

Anna Kate, who had a book about the famous frontiersman, nodded enthusiastically.

"Do you know how he met his wife, Rebecca?"

Anna Kate shook her head.

"Then let me tell you." Gabe began his story at once, painting with words a picture of a forest like this one, except in Tennessee, and a late-night hunt for food. He told how Davy spotted the glow of animal eyes in the shadowy brush, took aim at the "deer" he assumed he'd located, but for some reason couldn't bring himself to shoot. When the deer suddenly bolted, Davy pursued the sound of crashing tree limbs through the dense dark woods, wishing with every passing minute that he hadn't hesitated on the shot and lost his next meal. Then Davy stumbled onto a cabin, from which stepped a man with a rifle and a story of how his daughter, Rebecca, had just been chased through the woods by a panther.

"Who do you think the panther really was?" Gabe asked Anna Kate.

"Davy!" she exclaimed, adding with all seriousness, "and I'm sure glad he didn't shoot."

"Bet Rebecca was, too," Shari interjected with a dry laugh.

"Tell me another story," Anna Kate demanded.

"Just one a night," Jessi responded, getting quickly to her feet. She didn't want her daughter to be a pest. "We don't want Gabe to run out of tales, do we?"

"No...." Anna Kate didn't sound so sure.

"And it's almost ten o'clock, way past your bedtime anyway." Jessi reached out a hand to her daughter. "Hop up, kiddo. Time to hit the sack."

Grumbling, Anna Kate obeyed, and, after good-nights all round, she and Jessi walked hand-in-hand to their trailer.

"I'll be in shortly," Gabe called out just as Jessi reached the door.

She started at his words—she'd actually forgotten they were sharing living quarters—then covered up her faux pas by pasting a huge smile on her face and nodding at him. "Take your time." Please.

Stepping indoors, Jessi glanced around to gauge the intimacy of the trailer now that night enclosed it. Though actually fairly spacious with a good-sized kitchen-living room combination, a bedroom and a bathroom, it nonetheless seemed suddenly too small. Her feeling of claustrophobia intensified when Gabe stepped through the door just ten minutes later. She wasn't sure why, but credited his size, his personality, and his personal magnetism.

Or was her own repressed libido to blame?

Whatever, she thanked her lucky stars that they wouldn't be spending all that much time indoors. Gabriel Dillard could charm the pants—or was it pan*ties*—off her, for sure. Jessi just hoped he never figured it out. Her life was complicated enough.

"Come on, Anna Kate. Finish up your drink," Jessi said to her daughter, now seated on one of the bench seats at the built-in table and partaking of the milk-and-cookie snack that had been their bedtime ritual since the child had teeth. "Gabe is ready to turn in, and we're in the way."

"Take your time," Gabe said, echoing her earlier advice with a knowing grin. He tossed his hat onto the "couch" at the end of the trailer—it was really nothing more than a thick foam cushion about the width of a love seat—and slipped in opposite the table from Anna Kate before helping himself to a couple of cookies from the package.

Their table was much like a booth in a diner somewhere. Just looking at it, Jessi could hardly believe the whole thing converted into a bed. She suspected Anna Kate would be thoroughly intrigued once Gabe performed the makeover miracle and anticipated the child's begging to sleep there instead of on the normal bed she would share with Jessi in the other room for the duration of this trip.

"Would you like some milk?" Jessi asked Gabe, who was now munching on a second cookie.

"Yes, thanks," he answered around a mouthful of chocolate and marshmallow.

Jessi retrieved the milk jug from the refrigerator and

filled a glass to the top. Gabe drank it all in one long swallow, which earned him Anna Kate's admiration and an enthusiastic, "Do it again!"

He just laughed and, reaching across the table, tugged on her earlobe. "Want to help me turn this table into a bed?"

"We're gonna do *that?*"

"We are." Gabe got to his feet and motioned for Anna Kate to get to hers. While she did, he closed up the cookie package and handed it and the empty glasses to Jessi. Then he turned back to the table. "First you undo this," he explained to Anna Kate as he flipped open a fastener and then pushed the back of one bench seat forward.

Anna Kate did the honors on the other one.

"Good. Now we're going to pull this pin here—" he knelt down and demonstrated how the table pedestal could be lowered "—and see what happens?"

"Cool!" exclaimed Anna Kate, running her hands over the table top, now level with the folded-down seats.

"Next comes the good part." He opened a storage compartment over the love seat and extracted a rolled-up mattress, which he quickly straightened and situated on the foundation they'd made for it. Since a fitted sheet was already on the mattress, all he had to do was add a flat sheet, a couple of thermal blankets and a pillow. "And there you are. My bed."

"But I want to sleep in it!" Anna Kate argued, already hopping aboard to test it. "It's just my size, not yours."

"Maybe so, but you're going to sleep in the bedroom with me," interjected Jessi, already prepared for this battle. She used the tone that brooked no argument, and luckily Anna Kate didn't offer any, though her disappointment was evident as she climbed down and followed her mother to the opposite end of the trailer.

It was with much relief and a soft "good-night" to Gabe that Jessi firmly shut their bedroom door. Anna Kate pouted while they dressed in their nightclothes, but perked up a little when she realized she'd be sharing a bed with her mom, something Jessi didn't usually allow. Sleeping with Anna Kate was a little like sleeping with a whirlwind since she rolled all over the bed and took the blankets with her. Jessi doubted she'd get a decent night's rest this entire trip.

Finally, Jessi turned out the light. Intense darkness engulfed the room. Since no light showed around the edges of the door, Jessi assumed Gabe had turned in, too.

"When do I get to sleep in Gabe's bed?" Anna Kate asked rather loudly, breaking the silence.

"Maybe you can nap on it some afternoon." Jessi kept her voice low in hopes Anna Kate would follow her example.

No such luck. "But I want to at night." The words echoed off the walls.

"And just where do you think Gabe would sleep?" asked Jessi, quickly losing patience.

"With you."

"That's never going to happen."

"But, Mommy—"

"Goodnight, Anna Kate."

"Oh, goodnight." The child sounded quite miffed.

Jessi cherished the ensuing silence, which lasted maybe ten seconds.

"Heather's mommy and daddy sleep *together*." Anna Kate's tone accused and condemned.

"Good for them," Jessi retorted, ignoring her displeasure.

"Their bed has water in it."

Jessi sighed wearily and wished her night owl daughter would go to sleep. "Is that so?"

"Uh-huh. It's real bouncy, but Heather and me can't jump on it."

"I should hope not. They're not made for that."

"Heather's mommy and daddy do it all the time."

"They do?"

"Uh-huh." Anna Kate sat upright and peered down at

her mother, movement plainly visible since Jessi's eyes had finally grown accustomed to the dark. "Heather heard the water sloshing at night."

"Did she now..." Jessi murmured, trying not to laugh. Wouldn't Heather's parents just love to learn their daughter knew about their midnight acrobatics? "Well, *you* don't jump on it, okay?"

"Okay...but it's not fair, and Heather's *sooo* mad."

A chuckle, low and masculine, suddenly found its way through the paper-thin walls. Realizing Gabe had undoubtedly heard every word of this stimulating conversation and drawn the same conclusions she had, Jessi covered her head with her pillow.

She stayed in hiding until Anna Kate's even breathing indicated sleep, and unbroken silence at last reigned. Then and only then did Jessi put the pillow under her head and snuggle into her blankets. But sleep eluded her, thanks to an odd restlessness. Jessi felt empty, alone, almost as if longing for something or, heaven forbid, someone.

Was Gabe that some*one?* And was a life with him that some*thing?* Jessi thought not, though she did acknowledge their so-called marriage could undoubtedly be blamed for resurrecting some very old dreams she thought had died. Then there was the fact that, Stetson and boots aside, Gabe could claim many of the qualities she wanted in a mate.

But she'd been fooled before, so badly that it wouldn't matter if Gabe were perfect. Jessica Landers no longer sought a forever man and besides...this guy she'd married would get on her nerves before their short time together came to an end. Why, he'd even predicted it himself, hadn't he?

The next morning, Tuesday, Jessi rose before dawn to get busy with what she loved best: cooking. Studiously ignoring Gabe, who snored softly on his bed with his back to her, she silently went to work. Only when ham slices simmered on the stove and biscuits baked in the oven did she take a short break, slipping quietly outside and heading east to the cliff that Gabe had warned Anna Kate about. Jessi found it easily and sat on a boulder there to wait for the sun to raise its sleepy head over the mountainous horizon. The chill of the morning quickly penetrated her flannel shirt and jeans, and shivering, she began to frisk her arms.

"It's going to be a beaut today."

Jessi started at the sound of Gabe's voice, coming from somewhere behind her. Lost in appreciation of nature's coral, pink and gold light show, not to mention her warm-up efforts, she hadn't heard his approach.

"Yes, it is," she murmured, glancing back. With his tousled hair, bewhiskered jaw and tattered gray sweatpants, he looked as if he'd just rolled out of bed and out the door. "Do you always get up this early or did I wake you?"

"Actually both," Gabe told her, moving closer. He scratched his abdomen, part of which showed thanks to the stretched-out half T-shirt he wore. "I love to watch the sun rise, but today the smell of coffee and good food woke me." He glanced down at his clothes and gave her a lop-sided grin of apology. "Sorry about this, but I didn't want to take time to dress." Belatedly, he noticed the way she hugged herself. "You're cold."

"Doesn't matter," Jessi said, again briskly rubbing her arms. "I need to go in anyway." She got to her feet and gave the sunrise a last longing look.

At that instant, Gabe stepped up close behind and wrapped his arms over her upper body, an unexpected move that provided amazing warmth, yet made her shiver. If Gabe noticed her purely sexual response to his shockingly sensual attire, he didn't indicate it. Jessi was glad. The last thing she needed in her mellow mood was another proposition.

But had that first proposition, made at the restaurant, even been in earnest? Jessi had to wonder. Gabe had acted the perfect gentleman ever since...unless this gallant gesture, this body-to-body warm up, were some kind of come-on.

But no. Though admittedly a little turned on and tuned in to Gabe at the moment, Jessi could not blame him for her response. Any man who held her so tight would evoke the same emotions.

Wouldn't he...?

Minutes later, after the sun finally rose, Jessi headed back to the trailer, no closer to an answer to that burning question. Gabe walked with her, but once he turned his bed back into a table and grabbed up some clothes, he left again, leaving her to rescue the biscuits from the oven and prepare the scrambled eggs. Fresh fruit completed the menu, and just as Jessi set the last steaming dish on the table, August and Shari knocked on the door.

"Perfect timing!" Jessi greeted them.

"Thanks to a little nudge from our guide here," August told her, pointing to Gabe, who followed them inside the trailer.

Gabe now wore jeans and a plaid flannel shirt, plus heavy boots that thumped on the floor of the trailer with each step. He stashed his sleep clothes, all rolled up, under the couch.

"Where's little bit?" he asked, obviously referring to Anna Kate.

"I'll get her up later," Jessi answered, adding, "You know what a grump she is in the morning, especially if she can't watch cartoons while she eats."

"I do for a fact," murmured Gabe as if he'd lived with the girl for years and knew each and every bad habit.

"You can borrow our TV," Shari said as she slipped into the eating booth. August then sat next to her. "We don't get that many stations, but I'll bet you find some cartoons."

"Maybe later in the week," Jessi answered, determined not to steal her employer's television. She motioned for Gabe to sit across from the Taylors. "Until then, it might

be good for Anna Kate to do without it for a while. She's
an addict for sure.'' Jessi sat next to Gabe.

The four of them began to eat then, talking about the
weather, their plans for the day and whatever else leapt to
mind. This morning it wasn't hard for Jessi to pretend she
was really married to Gabe and simply on a camping va-
cation with friends.

It felt rather cozy until she remembered what marriage
really meant: loss...of identity, of freedom, and therefore
of happiness. Oh sure, men weren't all bad, but wasn't the
cost of owning one just too much to pay?

After the meal, the men headed outdoors to load up the
ATV's for their exploration. Jessi provided cold drinks and
a lunch, which Shari helped prepare. Mounting his ATV
and revving up its motor, Gabe felt like a cross between a
Hells Angel and Meriwether Lewis and wondered, not for
the first time, what he was doing so far from home on this
crazy treasure hunt.

But a job was a job, and heaven knew he needed every
cent of the big bucks he'd make from this one. A precious
young boy named Ryder Dillard waited patiently for Gabe
to provide him with a new life. Gabe could not, would not
let him down.

At eight o'clock, the men rode away from camp, Gabe
in the lead. He'd studied an area map for hours so had a
fair idea of where they were headed, but maps were man-
made and so sometimes less than perfect. Through the
years, Gabe had learned to rely on gut instinct and a sixth
sense so strong that at times he believed it qualified as
extrasensory perception.

Gabe had read up on ESP, trying to explain the premo-
nitions that had haunted him on occasion since childhood.
It was almost as if he had another self, maybe a more spir-
itual self, that knew all about the future and gave him hints
when he needed them most. He also experienced occasional
feelings he couldn't explain in the least—feelings of de-

spair, loneliness, and neglect that had nothing to do with his present life and almost felt secondhand. Weird stuff, this. And nothing he'd admit to anyone even though he'd come to accept it himself.

Would Gabe's mental openness prove helpful today? He hoped so. Though the woods were nice and the camping pleasant, Gabe wanted to do what Elaina had advised Jessi to do: take his money and run—straight to California and the boy who would turn his Washington house into a home.

"Could that be the ridge?" August's question sliced into Gabe's thoughts, reminding him he'd better concentrate on the task at hand instead of wishing it were over.

"Well, it isn't shaped like a panther, at least not in my opinion," Gabe answered, eyeing the rock mass August pointed out. "But it's not on the map, either, which makes it more of a possibility than the ridges that are."

August stared at him for a minute without speaking. "I get the feeling you think we're on a wild-goose chase."

"Let's just say I don't think we're going to find any kind of treasure in the caves on this map. They've all been explored who knows how many times before by hikers."

August considered that answer. "And that ridge—" he pointed to the rocks ahead "—isn't on your map?"

"No."

"Then let's see if we can find us a cave." He put his ATV in motion, leading the way deeper into the woods as Gabe followed.

The sun hovered just above the rocky horizon before the men returned to camp again. Though tired, they were both up emotionally, having found not one cave but a series of them, none of which were on Gabe's map. Hunger and the threat of impending darkness had sent them back to camp.

The minute they killed the engines on their vehicles and dismounted, Anna Kate ran up and grabbed Gabe's leg, almost knocking him over in her excitement at having them home again.

"What'd you find?" she asked, tipping her head back and eyeing him with those incredible violet eyes. She wore her hair in dog ears that curled every which way. Gabe laughed and playfully yanked on one of them.

"Nothing yet, but we might tomorrow."

At once Anna Kate released Gabe and dashed back toward the trailers. Only then did he notice that the women stood inside the dining tent, setting the table.

"Mommy! Mommy!" Anna Kate squealed as she darted into the tent. "Daddy G says they're going to find treasure tomorrow!"

August's soft laugh at the misinformation made Gabe turn and assess his employer, who seemed to have a weakness where the girl was concerned. That was lucky, Gabe thought. Anna Kate's enthusiasm could get on a man's nerves if he didn't like kids. Fortunately Gabe did, and so, it seemed, did August, though he probably wouldn't admit it.

Noting Gabe's scrutiny, August busied himself unloading the ATV, and it was without a smile that he headed to his trailer. That left Gabe wondering why the writer felt the need to appear so stern. Chalking it up to August's possible identity crisis, Gabe unloaded his own ATV and walked to the food tent.

Jessi and Shari met him at the flap that served as a door. As the blonde slipped past and made tracks to her husband to kiss him hello, Jessi grabbed Gabe's arm.

"You think you'll find something tomorrow?" Clearly she hoped they would.

Gabe didn't have to wonder why. He knew. "You mean you're already ready to ditch your hubby and go back to California?" he asked, keeping his voice low.

Jessi blushed and released him. "Well, I—"

"We did find some caves," Gabe interjected, letting her off the hook. "But didn't have time to explore them."

"I can tell you don't think you'll find anything." Now she looked more discouraged than embarrassed.

"The caves weren't on the map, which is good, but it's hard for me to believe some hiker hasn't already found and explored them. They weren't exactly hidden or even hard to get to."

"Oh." Clearly disappointed, Jessi turned back toward the picnic table, beautifully set for five.

"Am I such a horrible husband?" Gabe asked.

Jessi glanced toward the Taylors' trailer before replying. August and Shari stood in front of it, talking. "You're a fine husband...or will be to someone someday...I just...just..."

"Want to get on with your life?"

She sighed. "Something like that."

"So do I, and the sooner we hit pay dirt or give up on this site, the happier I'll be." Right now it seemed very important to Gabe that Jessi realize she wasn't the only one who had other things to do. Never mind that he found the idea of never seeing her and Anna Kate again a bit disturbing. That was to be expected of any man who valued friendships as much as he did...even after only a couple of days with Jessi and Anna Kate.

An awkward silence followed that comment, during which Gabe realized August and Shari now stared at him and Jessi. Was that an indication they were the topic of conversation? He had to wonder, thinking back over his behavior since his return to camp.

Had he greeted Jessi as a husband would?

Not by a long shot, Gabe realized, recalling the hello kiss Shari and her spouse had shared. Though August had actually removed marriage as a criterion for employment, Gabe wasn't comfortable confessing the lack of same now. No, the time to do that would've been when August first apologized for requiring a wedding. Since Gabe hadn't been truthful then, he certainly couldn't be now...at least not if he didn't want to look foolish.

"I probably should've kissed you when I got here, huh?"

"Excuse me?" Jessi's wide eyes conveyed her shock.

"A husband should kiss his wife when he gets home at night. Don't you agree?"

"I, um…" She looked at him and shrugged. "Actually, every couple is different."

"Well, I'm talking about us," Gabe said, a little amused by their dialogue. Clearly, he'd disconcerted her. "And I'd like to know if you want me to kiss you when I get back to camp in the evenings."

"*Want* has nothing to do with it."

Put in his place, Gabe sighed. "Okay, all right…let me rephrase that. Do you think I should kiss you when I get home at night?"

Jessi gave his question due consideration. "Probably."

"And what about when I leave in the mornings? Isn't a kiss in order then, too?"

"I really don't know."

"But you were married once, weren't you?"

"Yes."

"Did you kiss your husband goodbye in the mornings?"

"Sometimes I did; sometimes I didn't."

"What made the difference?"

"My frame of mind. We argued a lot. It's hard to kiss someone you're angry with."

"But when you weren't angry, you kissed him."

"Yes. My mother taught me that it brings good luck."

"Good luck? Then tomorrow we'll definitely kiss. As for now, I think it's a little late…I mean, I have been back for a good fifteen minutes."

"Yes, you have." She looked quite relieved by the fact.

"Of course, we could always kiss for some other reason."

"And what might that be?" Jessi asked, actually backing two steps away from him as if she already knew the answer and didn't care for it.

Gabe glanced toward his boss's trailer just in time to see

August, Shari and Anna Kate disappear inside it. "Actually there are several, but I was thinking of desire."

"Desire?" The word came out a panicked squeak.

Suddenly, the conversation lost its charm. "Damn, Jessi. I'm not going to jump your bones. I'm just going to kiss you."

"When?"

"Tomorrow morning, since I think if I tried it now, you'd scream or faint or something." He shook his head in disbelief of her low opinion of him. What had he done to earn it? "How about right before I leave camp?"

"That seems logical." She still looked rattled.

"Are you okay?"

"I'm fine…just a little nervous, I guess."

The thought of kissing him made her nervous? Now *that* hurt. "I passed my physical, Jessi. No communicable diseases."

"That's not the problem."

"Then what is?"

"It doesn't matter."

"Sure it does." He heard the squeak of an opening door and glanced toward the Taylors' trailer, to see August and Shari stepping out of it, Anna Kate and their television set in tow. Reaching out, Gabe caught Jessi by the shoulders. "Tell me quick…before they get here…or I'm going to kiss you now."

She clutched his biceps. "You wouldn't."

"Wanna bet?" he asked, slipping an arm around her waist, pulling her firmly against him. "Or would you rather just answer the question?"

"I'll answer it. I'll answer it…as soon as you let me go."

Gabe released her at once and pasted a smile on his face for the benefit of his employer, now mere steps away. "Why are you so damned nervous about one little kiss, Jessi?" Gabe asked, sotto voce.

"Because I'm afraid I won't want to stop with one," she whispered and then turned her back on him.

Chapter Five

Gabe could barely eat the meal Jessi had prepared, so stunned was he by her confession. Could he use it to his advantage? he wondered. Could he talk her into an affair that would soothe the aching need that consumed him every time he laid eyes on her?

Maybe, he realized. But wouldn't even a no-strings affair with a woman like Jessi be disastrous? She was a lady in every sense of the word, and he…well, he was a man without even so much as a name. They were a mismatch, and he knew from experience the complication and grief those could cause.

Besides…just because a woman admitted she might be interested in some experimental kissing, it didn't necessarily mean she wanted sex. Jessi had more sense than that, and Gabe had better—make that *smarter*—things to do, anyway.

The timing was wrong, all wrong, for romance.

"Are you finished?"

Jessi's question sliced into Gabe's thoughts. Glancing her way, he realized that he now sat alone at the table.

"Oh, uh, sure," he answered, leaping up. Outside the tent he saw August and Shari heading to the Dillard trailer, probably to help Anna Kate hook up her television.

Jessi took his half-empty plate and examined it. "You didn't like the roast?"

"I liked it fine," Gabe hastily assured her. "I just had some things on my mind and forgot to eat." He started for the opening of the food tent.

But Jessi caught his arm, stopping him. "What things?" she asked. "Did something happen in the woods today that I need to know about?"

"Nothing happened." At least, not in the woods.

"Then what's wrong?"

"Can't a guy skip a meal without getting the third degree?"

Gabe snapped, unwilling to admit where his thoughts had been for the last ten minutes.

"Well, ex-*cuse* me!" Jessi snapped right back. "I just thought you might want to talk about it."

"And that," Gabe told her, "is exactly what's wrong with marriage. Say 'I do,' and nothing's private anymore— not even your thoughts."

Jessi gave him a hard look and then, with a toss of her head, whirled and walked to a small table near the tent flap. The tilt of her chin, the square of her shoulders, even her brisk step revealed her irritation with him.

Gabe noted other things, too, as she noisily stacked the dirty dishes on a large tray, things he had no business noting, among them the length of her legs, the curve of her hips, the swell of her breasts. He closed his eyes, imagining what it would be like to slip up behind Jessi right this minute and press his needy body close. He'd hug her, that's what he'd do, and then curve his fingers around those beautiful breasts, testing their weight, teasing the tips to tautness, maybe even tasting them. That, of course, meant he'd have to help her out of her top and her bra, but Gabe didn't mind. Hell, he'd help her remove her jeans, too, and then get rid of his own clothes.

Oh, what sweet love they could make, he and Jessi. Sweet, sweet love the likes of which no well-matched husband and wife had ever experienced.

"Quit staring at me." Jessi sounded so irritated, Gabe wondered if she'd read his crazy thoughts.

"I'm not staring."

"Oh yes you are, and I want you to stop it."

"So not only do I now have to share my thoughts, I have to keep them clean as well?"

Jessi spun around to face him, her violet eyes wide and accusing. "What are you saying?"

"I'm saying that ever since your confession about the kiss, my mind has been in the gutter." He figured he might as well confess it—she was bound to notice his drooling sooner or later.

"You mean..." Visibly horrified, she couldn't even phrase her next question.

Gabe's spirits settled in his bootlaces even though he wasn't surprised she thought an affair was a bad idea, too. "You're a beautiful woman. I'm a red-blooded male. Of course I want you, but that doesn't mean you have to sleep with a gun. I may be a little rough around the edges, Jessi, but I respect you, and I know when I'm not wanted."

"I never said that," Jessi blurted, then tensed and clamped her mouth tightly shut, almost as if she wished she hadn't said *that*, either.

Gabe's jaw dropped. "You mean I *am* wanted?"

Jessi turned her back on him and busied herself with picking up the tray full of dishes instead of answering. Stepping in front of her, Gabe took her load.

"Answer me, Jessi," he said, words that drew her gaze to his.

She sighed and swiped her hands down her jeans. "Here's the deal, Gabe. You're a good-looking guy with a

lot of appeal. Naturally I'm feeling a certain…certain…"
She gave him a helpless look.

"Desire?" Gabe interjected hopefully.

Jessi shook her head. "More…*sexual curiosity,* actually,
but it's nothing personal."

"So any man would do?"

"Frankly, yes…if I was the kind of woman who followed impulse instead of reason. Fortunately, I'm not."

Gabe digested her frank words…or tried to. They didn't
sit all that well. "I don't know why I'm surprised that you
can resist me. I guessed that I wasn't your type the moment
we met."

"Type has nothing to do with my determination not to
get sexually involved with you. We're only married for the
moment, Gabe, and our situation is complicated enough
without throwing in sex."

"You do have a point," Gabe reluctantly admitted.

"So you'll quit staring at me like you were a minute
ago?"

"You mean as if I'd love to drag you off to a cave
somewhere and have my way with you?"

Jessi blushed. "Exactly."

"Then the answer is no."

Jessi's jaw dropped. "But I thought we agreed—"

"We agreed that sex is a bad idea *right now.* I'm not so
sure it might not be a great one later. Besides…all husbands
lust after their wives. That's what ensures procreation."

"I haven't seen August looking at Shari that way."

"Yeah, well, they do seem to have their problems,"
Gabe agreed even as the door to his trailer opened and the
couple in question stepped out into the crisp evening air.

"Shari told me that she really wants a baby, but August
thinks he's too old," Jessi whispered, picking up a stack
of plastic drinking cups.

"And that, my dear wife," Gabe muttered, "is exactly
the reason he's not staring at her. Staring leads to wanting,
which leads to getting, which leads to—"

"Babies."

"If you're not careful."

"And she might not be." They exchanged a speculative look, then Jessi led the way to the trailer, where August and Shari waited.

"The television is all hooked up," August said.

"And Anna Kate is trying it out," Shari added with a smile.

"Surprise, surprise," Jessi murmured, shaking her head as she opened the trailer door.

"Are you two interested in a campfire tonight?" Gabe asked.

"Actually I have some work to do." With a brisk nod, August moved toward his trailer.

"See you both in the morning," Shari told them and then hurried after her husband. Gabe and Jessi didn't make a move until the door of the Taylor trailer shut behind the couple.

Then Gabe stepped into his own humble dwelling—this house on wheels that seemed like a home whenever Jessi and Anna Kate were around. He walked at once to the counter, set down the loaded tray and began to fill the sink with water.

"You don't have to help," Jessi said as she joined him.

"I don't mind," Gabe answered. A quick glance around revealed that August had set up the television in the kitchen, undoubtedly because he thought this was where Anna Kate spent most of her time and even slept. "Anna Kate loves the TV, I see."

Jessi looked at her daughter, who had curled up on the love seat and now watched some syndicated sitcom. "Yes, and I suppose I should be grateful she's happy, though I was sort of hoping for some quality time with her while we're out here." She nudged Gabe out of the way and began to wash up the plastic cutlery, which she'd decided to reuse instead of throwing away like they did the paper plates and cups.

"As a single parent you don't get much of that, do you?" Gabe rinsed the forks she handed to him, sticking each in a plastic drainer once they were free of soap.

"Not as much as I'd like."

"It must be tough being both mom and dad."

"Yes…as you'll soon find out." Jessi gave Gabe a smile so sweet it took his breath away.

He swallowed hard. "Do you think I'm crazy to want Ryder? I mean, I've never even been a dad, much less a *single* dad."

"I think you're selfless, responsible, and incredibly kind. And I think you'll make Ryder a wonderful father. Of course it may take some practice—"

"Who's Ryder?"

Looking down, Gabe found that Anna Kate, who had apparently tuned in to their conversation and abandoned the television, stood beside him. Most of her hair, tousled by a day of play, had long since left the confines of her ribbons and now framed her face in curls. Gabe tugged on a particularly bouncy one and grinned at her.

"Ryder is my nephew. I'm going to adopt him, and then he will be my son."

Anna Kate's brows knitted in a frown. "What's 'dopt?"

"*Adopt* is when a grown-up takes home a kid who doesn't have a mom or dad and keeps him forever."

"Ryder doesn't have a mom or dad?"

"Not anymore."

"I don't have a dad anymore, either."

Gabe got rid of the plate he held, dried his hands on a dish towel, then reached for Anna Kate, scooping her up to set her on the counter near the sink. "Neither do I, though I've had two."

"Two!"

Gabe nodded.

Anna Kate eyed him with open curiosity. "Where are they?"

"I never met my real dad, so I don't know where he is.

My adopted dad died in Korea.'' Belatedly he remembered Anna Kate's age—too young to have had any geography lessons. ''That's a place a long way from here.''

''You were adopted, too?''

''That's right.''

''I wish I was.''

Gabe heard Jessi's sharp intake of breath. Surreptitiously, he grasped her by the wrist to silence whatever response she was about to make. ''Why?''

Anna Kate rolled her eyes in obvious disdain for his ignorance. ''So I could have a daddy, silly.''

''Anna Kate Landers!'' scolded Jessi, now distracted by the name her daughter had called her temporary stepfather. ''Where are your manners?''

''It's okay,'' Gabe told Jessi. He then turned back to the girl. ''Actually, you can't be adopted as long as you have a mom.''

''Why not?''

''That's just the way it works. No one can adopt you if your mom is doing a good job...unless she marries again, of course. Then her new husband can.'' Did that admittedly debatable truth make sense? Gabe wondered, anxiously watching Anna Kate's expression for some sign that she understood his bumbling explanation.

''Aren't you her new husband?'' Anna Kate asked, an astute question that evoked a soft groan from her mother and a wince from Gabe.

''Y-yes...''

''Then you can adopt me?''

Well hell. ''I—''

''Can't,'' Jessi interjected rather sharply, giving Gabe a look that warned him he'd said more than enough. ''He's already adopting Ryder. And besides, Gabe is just going to be my husband for a little while, remember?''

''I remember.'' Anna Kate sighed as if the weight of the world lay on her tiny shoulders.

''You know what I think?'' Gabe blurted. ''I think it's

time for Play-Doh.'' Luckily, he'd seen a package in the
pantry just this morning.

Anna Kate brightened at once, as did her mother. "We
have some?"

Jessi nodded and gave Gabe a grateful smile. "Hop
down and go sit at the table. We'll all three make something really wonderful…that is, if Gabe doesn't have other
things to do."

He shook his head and rescued Anna Kate from the
counter. She ran right to the table and crawled up on one
of the benches. Gabe sat on the other side. When Jessi
joined them a second later, modeling clay in hand, and tried
to sit next to her daughter, Anna Kate shook her head so
hard that what was left of her bedraggled ponytail became
airborne.

"Sit by Daddy G."

Jessi hesitated, then did as requested, no doubt to keep
the peace.

"May I catch what's left of the news?" Gabe asked,
pointing to the television at Anna Kate's elbow. Long forgotten, it played to no one.

The child nodded permission, and he began to change
channels until he found a station presenting the evening
headlines. Though the picture was a little fuzzy, the audio
sounded clear enough, and Gabe kept one ear on it while
he molded a blob of blue Play-Doh into a bear.

"Can you tell what this is?" he asked when both he and
the news were done.

"Mr. August?" Anna Kate ventured.

As amazed as he was amused by her reply—he'd already
forgotten comparing August to a bear—Gabe burst into
laughter. "Bingo! Now what are you making?"

"Guess," Anna Kate said, rolling a piece of yellow Play-
Doh into a long, skinny shape. She lay it gently on a pile
of similarly-formed pieces. "Toothpicks?" Gabe asked.

"No, sil—" Just in time Anna Kate caught herself and

glanced at her mother. "No. What do you think, Mommy?"

"A campfire?"

Anna Kate grinned and nodded vigorously. "What are you making?"

"Guess," Jessi answered, looking from one of them to the other.

Gabe eyed what she'd carefully fashioned, and knew at once what it was. He let Anna Kate guess, however.

"A Frisbee?"

"No," her mother answered even as her fingers shaped something else. She raised her gaze to Gabe, obviously waiting for him to offer a guess.

"A flying saucer?" he asked, purposefully missing the mark.

"That's half right," Jessi told him.

"I know! I know!" Anna Kate exclaimed, bouncing up and down in the excitement of discovery. "It's a saucer! And now you're doing a cup."

"Bingo!" Jessi's teasing grin said she'd borrowed Gabe's word on purpose. "And since we've all done things from this trip, why don't we make our whole camp in miniature?"

"I get to do the four-wheelers," Gabe said, raising his hand like some kid in school and waving it wildly.

Anna Kate rewarded his foolishness with a giggle.

"I'll do the food tent and the picnic table," Jessi said.

"And I'll do this camper." Anna Kate told them, grabbing up a chunk of the Play-Doh and working it into a new shape. Thanks to the ensuing silence, Gabe heard the familiar theme of a television show he hadn't seen in years. So did Anna Kate, who lit up like a Christmas tree.

"Gilligan! It's Gilligan!"

Clearly in kid heaven—fun TV *and* Play-Doh—Anna Kate enthusiastically pounded her colorful wad of dough and watched the antics of the *Minnow*'s stranded crew.

Gabe thought it rather timely that Gilligan and company

should be on right then. He felt a little lost from the world, himself. The good news was the fact that he liked his two partners-in-adventure. The bad was that he'd insulted one of them less than an hour ago.

Noting that Anna Kate had given the television all her attention, Gabe leaned close to Jessi and, putting his mouth to her ear, whispered, "I'm sorry."

"For which?" Jessi softly responded.

Was there that much to choose from? Gabe realized that maybe there was and could've kicked himself for being such a jerk. "For what I said out in the food tent. I swear I won't mention—" he glanced at Anna Kate, who appeared to be glued to the TV set, but might, as before, have an ear on this conversation "—s-e-x again. Okay?"

"Okay," Jessi responded. She sounded a little hesitant, and Gabe had to wonder why.

"Am I so hard to forgive?"

"You're easy to forgive," Jessi said, keeping her voice low and her eye on her daughter. "I was just wondering something."

"Don't wonder. Ask."

Jessi eyed Anna Kate, then, motioning to Gabe to come along, slipped out of the booth, walked over to the cabinet and opened it as though searching for something. "Was that just testosterone talk earlier?"

"I'm not sure what you mean."

"Would you say the things you said to any woman, or are you really attracted to me, myself…?"

Now where is this headed? Gabe wondered. "I've been divorced for ten years and have dated maybe six, seven women in all that time, none of them more than twice. You're the first woman I've propositioned, so it's definitely you."

"Oh." She retrieved a couple of plastic drinking cups from the cabinet and turned to Anna Kate. "Ready for milk and cookies?"

The child, caught up in her television program, didn't

reply, sure indication she really wasn't listening to her mother and Gabe. Jessi glanced at her watch, obviously noting how early it was, and shifted her gaze to Gabe. "Thirsty?"

"No, but I am curious."

"About what?"

"About why you're checking out my motives. Care to enlighten me?"

"Not really."

"But you will...."

"Only if I must."

"You must. I've been honest with you."

Jessi nodded. Setting down the cups, she turned her back on them, leaned against the counter and crossed her arms over her chest, a defensive position if Gabe ever saw one. "I believe I've already confessed a certain sexual curiosity about you."

"Actually, you said it had nothing to do with me."

"And, actually, I lied."

Gabe caught his breath. "So sex with me doesn't sound all that bad?"

"No." She sighed. "You told me you were a red-blooded male. Well, I'm a red-blooded female, and being such, I like sex okay."

Okay? She only liked sex *okay?* Gabe frowned. Her ex must have been some lousy lover. Or maybe he'd simply never taken the time to show Jessi how pleasurable sex could be. What an idiot, Gabe decided, knowing for certain that he'd take his time with Jessi if ever given the chance. She was a woman worthy of long kisses and lazy loving.

Loving? Gabe tensed at the thought. Not that, he quickly but silently amended. Never that. Loving, in his experience, meant losing, be it dad, wife or sister. Gabe had loved and lost enough for one lifetime. No, he meant lazy *exploration*...of Jessi's body, mind and soul until he knew the woman so well he could anticipate her every desire.

"So you understand there's no need for an apology?" Jessi asked.

Gabe tuned in to her again with effort. "Yeah."

"And you understand why we can't really do anything, even though we're both fairly willing?"

Fairly willing? Gabe swallowed back a laugh. *She* might be fairly willing. *He* was more gung ho. "I understand."

"Good." She looked vastly relieved and started back to the table.

Gabe caught her by the arm. "Wait. I want to ask you something."

"Okay." Now she looked wary.

"I know next to nothing about you—your family, your first marriage. How about answering a few questions?"

"All right then."

"Are your parents living?" Gabe asked.

"No. Mother died four years ago. Dad died two years before that. They were both in their eighties. I'm the last of five children, and was born to them rather late in life."

"Where are your brothers and sisters?"

"New Mexico, Arizona, Maine and Indiana." She counted the states off on her fingers, then gave him a smile. "Are you sure you aren't thirsty?"

"Well, maybe. What kind of juice do we have?" Stepping over to the miniature refrigerator, Gabe opened the door and perused the contents. When he saw a jug of apple cider, he retrieved it and turned back to Jessi. "I guess you have lots of nieces and nephews, huh?"

"Lots *and* lots," she answered, pouring a tumbler full for Gabe and then herself.

He drank some, then stood in thoughtful silence, suddenly aware of how little family he had. "I envy you all those relatives. But most anyone without any would, I guess."

"Oh, I don't know about that," Jessi answered and then sipped her own drink. "My ex-husband had no one but his mother, and he hated all my kith and kin."

"Speaking of that ex...tell me something about him," Gabe said, glad she'd provided him with such a smooth transition to his next inquisition topic.

Jessi wrinkled her nose with distaste at the choice. "What do you want to know?"

"His name. What he did for a living. Where you two lived. How often you had sex."

"What did you say?" She stared at him over the top of the plastic cup she'd raised to her lips.

Ruing that last question, which had tumbled off his tongue quite by accident, Gabe asked, "I asked his name."

"Oh. Les Landers."

"What did he do for a living?"

"He repaired televisions, VCRs, radios...that sort of thing."

"And the two of you lived...?"

"In an apartment in Sun Bay."

"You were cooking at the time?"

"Actually, I was waitressing at a gourmet restaurant. That's where I got interested in cooking, and where I met Les, who loved good food, especially if someone else was paying for it." She grimaced.

"So what happened between you and the TV repairman?"

Jessi looked at Anna Kate, still entranced by the television, before she replied. "Nothing after the newness wore off—probably the reason we split. We shared little honest affection and less chemistry. Loyalty was lacking, too, which is why he left when he realized how very little we actually had in common. The marriage was a big mistake that I really can't explain, and I was not sorry when he left...at least for myself. I wish he'd done better by Anna Kate."

"He never sees her?"

"Never, nor does he pay child support even though I've taken him back to court twice. After the last time he left the country. I haven't heard from him since and don't expect to.''

Gabe shook his head and glanced Anna Kate's way, full of sympathy. How on earth could men abandon their children? he wondered, enjoying the magic of her laughter. Especially children as exceptional as Anna Kate and Ryder?

''As for the sex question...''

Gabe started guiltily and shifted his attention back to Jessi, who looked him dead in the eye.

''We had it often enough for me to wonder what it would feel like if I were really in love with the man. Now I think I've answered all your questions, so how about your answering a few of mine?''

Annoying...but only fair. ''Fire away.''

''How often did you and *your* ex have sex?'' Jessi asked, eyes twinkling with mischief.

''Every time I could talk her into it,'' Gabe confessed with a dry laugh.

''So she never initiated it?''

''Do women ever?'' Gabe countered. In his admittedly limited experience, they didn't.

''I believe *I* might....'' The twinkle in her eyes had dimmed, and she looked almost wistful and quite serious. ''If I had the right man, that is. In fact, I don't think I'd ever get enough of him.''

Sexier words had never been spoken. Suddenly wishing he were that ''right man,'' Gabe took a long swallow of his drink, then set the empty tumbler in the sink.

Turning back to Jessi, he murmured, ''Lucky guy.''

''Why, thank you, Gabriel.''

Feeling oddly choked up, Gabe walked over to the eating booth and sat across from Anna Kate again. He heard the Gilligan theme play once more, and realized that the show had ended. Anna Kate's regretful sigh confirmed it.

''Aren't you finished yet?'' Gabe teased, looking pointedly at the chunk of Play-Doh she held.

Anna Kate looked down at the unformed mass and giggled, then shook a finger at him. "Aren't you?"

Gabe grinned, snatched up the Play-Doh and began to roll out a wheel of the ATV he'd said he would make. He worked so quickly that his fingers fairly flew. Noting that, Anna Kate laughed and began to race him. Jessi soon joined in the fun, and less than an hour later they were admiring a miniature campsite.

Though the proportions weren't perfect—the bear could've eaten the campers in one huge gulp—Gabe, Jessi and Anna Kate congratulated one another on their efforts. Then Jessi gave Anna Kate her milk and cookies.

Finally, Gabe's watch said nine o'clock. Apparently Jessi's did, too, since she put her daughter's empty glass in the sink and motioned for her to crawl out of the booth. Anna Kate obeyed with a telling yawn and followed her mom all the way to the bedroom door, only to run back and scramble onto the bench seat occupied by Gabe.

"Give me a kiss," the child demanded, on her knees and leaning close.

Gabe did as requested, placing the kiss on the tip of her uptilted nose.

"Now give my mommy one," Anna Kate next said.

Not a bit tempted to argue, Gabe nudged Anna Kate off the bench and then followed suit. Standing, he beckoned to Jessi, who just shook her head.

"Don't you think now is a better time for the first one instead of tomorrow, in front of our employer?" Gabe asked.

Jessi tensed, thought for a minute, then walked back to him.

Gabe took her by the shoulders, tugged her a step closer and then dipped his head to place a kiss on her cheek.

"On the mouth!" Anna Kate as good as shrieked, clearly outraged. "Heather's daddy kisses her mommy on the mouth...like this." The girl closed her eyes, tipped her head back and held out her arms—melodramatic movements that made Jessi's eyes widen with shock. Then Anna Kate parted her lips.

Jessi grabbed the table for support, and pressed the other hand to her chest as though holding back a heart attack. "Oh my goodness..." She raised a panicked gaze to Gabe, who tried to look properly shocked, but wound up laughing.

"So that's how they do it, huh?" he murmured.

Anna Kate opened her eyes and nodded vigorously.

"Then we'll give it a go," he announced, pulling Jessi into his embrace and dipping her way back, as if he were a dashing sheikh and she his swooning harem girl. He did it more to tease Anna Kate than anything. And the child rewarded him with a squeal of encouragement, even as Jessi hung on for dear life, her face inches from Gabe's, and tried to regain her footing.

"What on earth are you do—?" Jessi got no further.

Unable to resist the close-up of her lips, so conveniently pursed, Gabe gave in to his need and laid a noisy smooch right on them.

Chapter Six

Jessi's heart pounded; her knees turned to jelly; her head swam. Totally off balance by the time Gabe ended the shocking kiss and set her back on her feet, she actually stumbled and might have landed on her bottom if he hadn't been quick and pulled her up tight again.

"How was that?" Gabe asked Anna Kate, his words warm against Jessi's hair.

The four-year-old just giggled in response and, clearly delighted with the way things had gone, skipped the five steps to the bedroom. Jessi watched until she vanished through the door, then shifted her gaze to Gabe...or tried to. Close as he was, he looked blurry. But she knew who held her so tight. Oh yes, indeed.

Gabe's body, pressed to Jessi's, felt rock solid and sturdy. She relished the sensation of his considerable male strength. How nice it would be to lean on this capable man, she thought, to let him take a share of the load she'd borne alone for so long. He was the type of person who'd do that...who'd be there when times got tough, who'd help make decisions, who'd ease her burden.

But wasn't turning her life over to a man exactly what she'd promised herself she would never do again?

Of course it was.

So even if he loved her, and their marriage wasn't a fraud, she'd never let go entirely. She'd paid too high a price for her current independence.

Running her hands lightly down Gabe's shoulders, biceps and then forearms, Jessi grasped him by the wrists and tugged his arms loose of their embrace.

"Don't you dare do that in front of the Taylors," she said to him as she put precious inches between them.

"Why not?" Gabe acted as if he honestly didn't know.

Although sure that he *did* know, Jessi nonetheless enlightened him. "Married people do not kiss that way...at least not in public."

"So you want me to save the theatrics for our private times?" He sat at the table again, his gaze steady and a bit disconcerting.

"I want you to save the theatrics, period. You're playing with fire, Gabe."

"Don't I know it," he murmured, the next second shaking his head as if to clear it. "You do something to me, Jessi girl. You make me forget what I need so that I wind up focusing on what I want."

"I'm not a girl," Jessi retorted, moving toward the bedroom door. "Anna Kate is a girl. I'm a woman...a woman who knows exactly what it will take to make her happy and has plans to get it. You, Mr. Dillard, are not on my must-have list, just as I'm not on yours. We'd do well to remember that."

"Amen," Gabe murmured, looking decidedly sheepish.

"So there'll be no more of this funny business...no matter what Anna Kate says?"

Gabe held up a hand as if taking an oath in court. "I swear."

Jessi nodded her satisfaction. "Good night, Gabe."

"Good night," he answered.

Gabe's gaze swept her from head to toe as it had so many times since they met. Feeling thoroughly touched, Jessi turned her back on him and retreated into the bedroom. Then firmly, with great relief, she shut the door to any and all temptation.

Wednesday morning, following another early breakfast, Gabe and August loaded their lunches, some water and their gear onto the ATV's. Gabe kissed Jessi goodbye as planned, but thankfully not as practiced. The last thing she needed after a night of embarrassingly erotic dreams about her new husband was another no-holds-barred kiss. August and Shari might find themselves astonished witnesses to an impromptu honeymoon, begun right there on the breakfast table.

As it was, she barely kept her cool when their lips brushed that morning. Watching Gabe vanish into the woods seconds later, Jessi could only stare after him and wonder at his power over her. No other man had affected her this way, not even her husband. What was Gabe's secret?

"I hope they find something today," Shari murmured, rubbing her arms to warm them against the chill in the autumn breeze. That same breeze kept the trees in motion, resulting in a constant shower of leaves in all shapes and hues. It would be a sight around noon when the sun shone high overhead and the various colors came to life.

"Tired of the great outdoors already?" Jessi asked, responding to the longing in Shari's voice.

The blonde shrugged. "Things haven't gone the way I expected."

"What do you mean?" Jessi asked, curious.

"I thought this return to the basics would make a difference in August, in our marriage."

"And it hasn't?"

"No. He's so caught up in his quest for fame that he hasn't even noticed the change in scenery." Shari stared into the woods. "I pictured the two of us lying under a canopy of stars each night, nothing on our minds but each other." She laughed without humor and gave Jessi a sheepish smile. "Instead, he spends his spare time poring over those stupid treasure maps of his, dreaming about a pot of gold at the end of some rainbow that doesn't even exist." She shook her head and headed into the trailer. "If I'd only known…"

"What?" Jessi asked, following her indoors.

"That he was going to have a midlife crisis." Shari sat at the table and picked up her mug. Jessi went to the stove and retrieved the coffee pot to give them a warm-up.

"You wouldn't have married him?" Jessi asked, turning to refill Shari's mug and then her own.

Shari laughed as though that were the most ridiculous thing she'd ever heard and played with the huge diamond mounted on her wedding ring. "Oh, I'd have married him, all right—you can't deny your destiny—but I'd have had a baby right away instead of waiting."

Jessi thought about that as she slipped into the booth opposite Shari. "You honestly believe August is your destiny?"

"Why, yes," Shari murmured, taking a sip of the hot coffee. Her gaze locked with Jessi's over the rim of the mug. "Just as Gabe is yours. Or don't you believe in that?"

"Actually, I never thought about it much."

"Yet you married Gabriel."

"Yes."

"Why?" Shari asked, and then laughed somewhat sheepishly. "As if I wasn't married to the reason why. I guess what I'm asking is what drew you to Gabe in the first place?"

Jessi hesitated for reasons Shari couldn't possibly understand.

"Please indulge me," the blonde said. "I've thought about this a lot, and I have a theory I'm sure is the right one."

"But I've been drawn to men before, you know, and even married one of them. None were my destiny."

"Ah, but do you know what drew you to those other men?"

"Yes."

"Each one of them?"

"Yes."

"And Gabe," Shari said, drinking the last of her coffee. She shook her head when Jessi started to get up and get the pot for another refill. "Do you know what drew you to him?"

It's *draws,* not *drew,* Jessi wanted to scream. Instead, she murmured, "I haven't a clue."

"And there you have it!" Shari exclaimed with a smile of triumph. "When we can't explain why we want a man, it's because he's our destiny."

Jessi stared at her in disbelief.

"Oh, don't you get it?" Shari asked, obviously mistaking Jessi's doubts for misunderstanding.

Jessi shook her head. "I'm afraid I don't."

"If we're attracted to some guy for a recognizable reason, be it his cute butt, his money or even his job, we're using our conscious minds, right?"

"I suppose so."

"You *know* so," Shari retorted. "And that means if we're drawn to a man for no recognizable reason, if we, in fact, doubt our sanity in choosing him, then we're using our subconscious minds. Now, which mind is the smartest…subconscious or conscious?"

"I don't know."

"Then let me put this another way. Which do you trust most? Instinct or reason?"

"Instinct," Jessi answered without hesitation.

"So do I. And my instinct drew me to August, just as yours has drawn you to Gabe." She sat back. "Tell me I'm right. Go ahead, tell me."

How on earth had the conversation taken such a turn?

Jessi wondered even as she said the words Shari wanted to hear. "You're right."

"And Gabe is your destiny?"

"Perhaps." When Shari rolled her eyes in exasperation, Jessi could only shrug and picture Gabe as he'd looked when he left—faded jeans, olive green T-shirt, light camouflage jacket, that cowboy hat.

Her destiny? That rugged, outdoors kind of guy. Surely not.

At that moment the bedroom door opened and a sleepy-eyed Anna Kate walked into the kitchen dressed in her nightshirt. Pleased to see her daughter, who was a welcome interruption to the crazy destiny discussion, Jessi scooped her up and kissed her good morning.

"Hungry?"

Anna Kate nodded.

"What would you like to eat?"

"Messy eggs."

"With toast and butter?" Jessi asked.

Anna Kate nodded, yawned and cuddled against her mother.

"Messy eggs?" Shari looked so bewildered that Jessi had to laugh.

"That's what she has always called scrambled eggs. Fried eggs are 'neat' and boiled eggs are 'roll-y.'"

Shari sat upright in the booth. "Scrambled eggs and toast are my specialty, remember?" She slid off the bench seat to stand next to Anna Kate. "May I make your breakfast today?"

Clearly intrigued by the idea, Anna Kate nodded.

Shari, a huge smile on her face, got right to work.

Though the women didn't expect their men to get home before dark that night, the ATV's—actually only *one* of the ATV's—roared back into camp around one o'clock. August and Gabe were both aboard, along with a tire, strapped on the rear rack. Jessi and Shari sprang from their respective trailers and rushed forward to greet the men, neither of whom looked happy.

"What happened?" Shari demanded before August even had time to kill the engine. "Are you guys okay?"

"It's just a flat, Shari." He sounded quite irritated.

They'd had to leave the other ATV in the woods. No wonder they looked so out of sorts.

"Do we have a spare?" Jessi asked Gabe as August got off the ATV.

"Nope." Tossing the tire to the ground, Gabe swung a leg over the seat and dismounted.

"What are you going to do?" Jessi asked, catching his arm in her hand.

"Drive in to the nearest town and see if I can get it repaired or buy another."

"How far away is that?" Jessi couldn't remember.

"About twenty-five miles. Do you need anything?"

"Actually, I do. May I come along?"

Gabe nodded and turned to Shari and August. "What about you two? Want me to get anything while I'm in town?"

"A newspaper," August answered.

"And something chocolate," added Shari.

Gabe glanced back at Jessi. "Where's Anna Kate?"

"Napping."

"I'll watch her," interjected Shari. "You two go on."

Without another word, Gabe picked up the tire and strode to his truck. He lifted the hatchback of the camper top and tossed it in. Jessi dashed indoors, grabbed her purse, then joined him. Minutes later they were on a two-lane highway, headed north.

"Did you get to explore the cave at all?" Jessi asked, eyeing the man whom Shari considered her destiny.

"Empty."

That word said it all and more.

"So we're back to square one."

"Yep."

With a sigh, Jessi looked out the windows and tried to enjoy the scenery. It wasn't that hard to do, thanks to the mountains, the colorful trees and even the blue sky. The sunshine streaming in Gabe's window revealed he had blond streaks in his light brown hair, and reaching out to examine a stray lock, Jessi marveled that she'd never noticed the two-tone shade.

"Did you have this done?" she couldn't resist teasing.

"What?"

"Did you have your hair streaked?"

"My hair is not streaked," Gabe replied with a snort.

"Oh yes it is," Jessi answered, singling out one very light hair and yanking it free of his scalp.

"Ow!" Gabe exclaimed, vigorously rubbing a spot on the back of his head. The movement knocked his cowboy hat forward.

"Don't be such a baby," Jessi scolded, setting the hat straight and then showing Gabe the decidedly blond hair she'd borrowed from him. And guessing he'd never used a hand mirror to see the back of his head, Jessi wasn't surprised that he didn't know about the streaks. "See there? Blond."

Gabe eyed it. He then took off his hat and glanced in the rearview mirror. His hair, at least in front, looked quite dark. "Maybe it's gray."

"No, it's blond," Jessi answered, adding, "Sun did it, I'll bet."

Gabe looked quite relieved to have solved the mystery. "Yeah. Sure. That makes sense."

Jessi had to laugh, and when she did, Gabe laughed too…and then nearly ran off the pavement. Gabe corrected that with a sharp turn of the steering wheel.

"Maybe you'd better keep your eyes on the road," Jessi suggested.

"And maybe you'd better sit closer so I can," Gabe retorted, patting the seat next to him.

When Jessi hesitated, Gabe released her seat belt, lay a

hand on her knee and tugged. Thanks to the vinyl seat, shiny and slick, Jessi slid right over until their thighs touched. Gabe then lay an arm across her shoulders.

"What are you doing?" Jessi had to ask. Though she liked the new arrangement, she doubted the wisdom of it.

"We're supposed to be newlyweds, alone for the first time in days. I'm trying to look convincing."

"But nobody's watching us."

"You don't know that," Gabe told her.

Jessi glanced all around. "There isn't another car or human being in sight anywhere. Of course, the road does curve rather sharply, so we can't see what lies ahead, but the chances of anyone we might see running to tell August that we're hugging the doors instead of each other is really—"

"Jessi!"

She started. "What?"

"Would you please shut up and for once, just this once, not analyze the situation?"

Offended, Jessi clamped her mouth tightly shut and gave him a stiff nod.

Gabe sighed. "Now I've made you angry."

She didn't answer.

"I didn't mean to. I only…I mean, I just…." He sighed again and removed his arm from around her so he could grasp the steering wheel with both hands. "Bad idea. Forget it."

The ensuing silence was broken only by the hum of the tires on the road and soon became awkward. Jessi wished she'd just kept her mouth shut a few minutes ago instead of trying to justify her pleasure at being held so close.

She blamed her babbling on Shari's cockeyed theory about destiny. Already one to over-analyze a given situation, Jessi guessed she would now dissect every emotion in some misbegotten search for reasons that would mean Gabe *wasn't* her destiny.

"I'm sorry," she told Gabe.

"I'm sorrier," he answered with a slow shake of his head. "I know I agreed to keep my distance, but to-day...well, today I guess I could use a hug."

At once Jessi's heart went out to him. "Bad morning?"

"The worst," Gabe agreed.

Without further thought, Jessi put her arms around his neck and gave him the requested hug. She then rested her cheek on his shoulder. "Let's forget all about August Taylor and his treasure hunt and just enjoy this outing, okay?"

"Absolutely."

"Does this radio work?" She reached out and punched the power button to see for herself. The sound of static filled the truck, but Jessi soon found a station playing soft rock. "This okay?"

"Perfect," Gabe told her.

Jessi doubted that. The CDs lying in the in-dash storage box all featured country music. Nonetheless, when an old James Taylor song came on seconds later, Gabe whistled along, proof he hadn't lied.

"Do you always tell the truth?" Jessi asked.

Gabe tensed. "Yes...well, almost always. I have been known to pull a leg or two, but only in fun."

"So when it's important, you're honest?"

"Bingo." He frowned at her. "Why?"

"I have a question to ask you, and I want the straight truth."

"All right." He sounded a bit hesitant.

Letting go of Gabe, Jessi sat up straight again and tried to formulate her confusion into a logical question.

"Better buckle up," Gabe said, breaking into her concentration.

Automatically, Jessi obeyed, retrieving the middle belt and sliding the buckle into the latch. She tightened it with a single pull. "Here's my question. Do you believe in destiny?"

"You mean fate?"

"I suppose they're the same thing."

"Then no, I don't."

"So what's your theory?"

"I believe fate is really nothing more than the result of choices. From birth, we make decisions, and each of those decisions results in another until we are what we are."

"For example...?"

"I decided to leave home at an early age even though I didn't have a job skill or money. As a result, I had to take any work I could get, and as a result of that I met Jerry Clark."

"Your friend in Washington."

Gabe nodded.

"But what about your real parents abandoning you? And what about your adoptive father's untimely death? Those weren't a result of choice."

"Not *my* choice, no. But certainly their own."

"So our choices intersect with other people's choices? And when bad things happen, it's just because someone somewhere made a poor decision?"

Gabe slapped a hand on the steering wheel. "Exactly."

"That makes sense, I suppose, but while it's true we're a product of our choices, I have to wonder if fate isn't what makes everyone's decisions crisscross so dramatically."

Gabe kept his eyes on the road, which had straightened out and leveled noticeably. "So even though it was August's decision to call Elaina, and her decision to call us, and our decision to take the jobs, *fate* brought us all together?"

"Maybe. August could have called someone besides Elaina, you know, and she could've found any number of other cooks and guides. We could've had other obligations, too. But none of us did."

Gabe sat in thoughtful silence. "You realize that if what you say is true, you're my destiny."

Jessi caught her breath. "Oh, I don't think so."

"But you just said—"

"I was talking nonsense." She pasted a smile on her

face and wished she'd never brought up this troubling topic.
But Shari's theory had disturbed her, and talking out confusion was always the best way to alleviate it. "Sorry about
that. I don't know why I'm so...so...*analytical* today. Must
have something to do with all this time I've suddenly got
on my hands."

"That'll do it," Gabe solemnly agreed.

The conversation stayed safely neutral for the next
twenty minutes. At that time, Gabe began to slow the truck
to match the speed limit posted on the sign they'd just
passed. About a half mile further, there was an even lower
limit posted, sure indication they neared civilization.

Two minutes later, a town called Neely Bend came into
view. Gabe pulled up to a gasoline station and stopped the
truck. He and Jessi both got out, and while he took care of
the tire, she walked to the road and inspected what must
be the main drag of this town, population three hundred
and fifty, according to a welcome sign.

To her left, north, she saw a store of some kind, a café,
and a church, and, to her right, a beauty shop. That was it.
Neely Bend, in total. There were a couple of cars parked
near the store, and Jessi saw one or two people standing
outside it. Charmed, Jessi glanced back toward the station
to find that Gabe had handed over the damaged tire and
now walked her way.

"Joe, there—" he indicated the station attendant
"—says he'll be done in a half hour. Want to do your
shopping while we wait?"

"Sure," Jessi answered. Together they walked to a
brick-and-wood building with a sign on it that said Pap's
Place. Though Jessi had her doubts about the store having
anything much, once inside, she changed her mind.

The store had at least one of everything, or that's how it
looked anyway. Merchandise filled the shelves, the aisles,
the doorways and even hung from the ceiling. Jessi spotted
the grocery section right away. Heading in that direction,

she picked up one of the carrying baskets provided for customers, and began to peruse the goods.

Gabe headed toward the tools, but when he joined her again some time later, he didn't have a tool at all, but a stuffed teddy bear and a baseball cap.

"And what are those?" Jessi asked him, as she unloaded her grocery items on the checkout counter at the back of the store.

"A bear for Anna Kate and a cap for Ryder," Gabe answered. "Think Anna Kate will get the joke?"

"I do."

"I'd like to mail this cap to Ryder. Maybe a card, too." He glanced toward the front door and the plate glass windows next to it. "Wonder where the post office is...?"

"To your right," answered the old man busy ringing up Jessi's purchases. With a nod, he indicated a corner of the store heretofore unexplored by either Jessi or Gabe. Turning, she saw another counter, alphabetized bins for mail, and the standard blue-and-red mailbox with a slot on one side and a hinged door on the other.

"You the postmaster?" Gabe asked. Jessi could see that his amusement matched her own.

"Yes, and I'll be with you in a jiff." He grinned. "Name's Pap Mason, by the way. I'm store manager, postmaster, and husband to Eula Dale Mason, owner of that café down the street. You'll want to try her apple pie while you're in town. It's the best in six counties."

"Maybe we'll do that, Mr. Mason. I'm Gabriel Dillard. This is Jessi Lan—uh, Dillard, my wife."

Jessi smiled at Pap Mason, who nodded.

"Newlyweds?"

Jessi blinked in surprise. "How could you tell?"

"Those shiny rings...plus the fact that Gabe here forgot your new name." He chuckled as if that were the funniest thing that had happened in days. Jessi guessed it might be.

True to his word, Pap, who wore denim overalls and a bright red shirt, soon handed Jessi a bagful of groceries.

After Gabe paid for his bear and cap and bought a postcard, Pap found him a box, then led the way to the post office counter. There, he provided Gabe with a pen for filling out the postcard and tape for sealing the box. Once the cap was securely packaged, Pap sold Gabe proper postage and a label, which Gabe addressed.

Just under an hour after they entered Pap's Place, Jessi and Gabe left the store. They walked slowly back to the gasoline station, Jessi carrying the bear and Gabe the grocery bag, into which he'd put August's newspaper and Shari's chocolate bar.

Pleased that Gabe had remembered their employers' requests, Jessi examined her daughter's fluffy brown teddy bear. "Anna Kate is going to love this, but it probably wasn't such a good idea to buy it."

"Because she might name it August?" Gabe asked.

Jessi laughed and shook her head. "No, because she might love you even more than she already does, which, I think, is too much." She slipped her arm through his. "This daddy-on-loan deal has the potential for heartache. In fact, it's like finding and feeding a stray puppy, only to have the owner show up and claim it."

"I remind you of a stray puppy?" He feigned outrage.

"That's not what I meant, and you know it," she retorted, lightly slapping his arm.

Gabe grinned, but that expression didn't last long. Stopping short, he turned to Jessi. "Maybe I should take the bear back."

"Oh, don't do that."

"But I don't want to hurt her...."

"It can be a reminder of the fun you two had together."

Though obviously not too sure about that, Gabe nonetheless resumed walking to the station. Once there, they learned that Joe, who was just a teenager, couldn't find the leak and so he had called the owner to come help. Since the two of them now labored over the tire, Gabe bought Jessi and himself a soft drink, then sat with her on a cracked vinyl bench in the garage, about ten feet from the men. She could smell gasoline and motor oil.

"You're awfully quiet," Gabe commented. "Still worried about the teddy bear?"

"No, but I am worried about this treasure hunt," Jessi answered, keeping her voice low. "I mean, how will you know whether you've found the right cave and it was just empty, or you simply found the wrong cave?"

"I'm not sure we will," Gabe admitted. "But I will tell you the same thing I told Taylor yesterday. The Panther Ridge we're looking for is probably not on any map."

"Panther Ridge? You two are looking for Panther Ridge?" The question came from the station owner, who had Tinker sewed on his shirt. He sported a handlebar mustache and looked to be as much of a character as Pap.

"What I'm looking for is a ridge shaped in some way like a panther. I think the name *Panther Ridge* is a local one, maybe very old. I don't expect it to be on a map."

"What are you going to do once you get there?" asked Roger, eyeing them curiously.

"A photo shoot. I'm a photographer. She's a model."

Jessi nearly fell off the bench. And he called himself *honest*.

"The owner of the fashion magazine we work for heard about a place called Panther Ridge, and he wants photos of her on this ridge for next month's edition."

"No kidding...." Tinker eyed Jessi as if she came from another planet.

She squirmed under his appraisal and tried to look glamorous, barely managing a stiff smile. Then, casually laying her arm along the back of the bench, she pinched Gabe really hard through his thick cotton shirt.

He jumped, then tried to cover it by getting suddenly to his feet and strolling casually toward Joe and Tinker. "Know of any place around here with a ridge shaped like a panther's head or body or—?"

"Tail?" Jessi interjected somewhat wryly.

"Not around here." Tinker bounced the finished tire on the concrete floor. "My gramps used to hunt at a place called Panther Ridge about two hours from here. Don't know if it's the one you want or not, but it might be worth a try."

"Can you show me on the map?"

"I can get you within a mile or so, I think." He motioned Gabe to come closer, then lowered his voice and said something Jessi couldn't catch. Curious, she got to her feet and walked over to them, but by the time she got there, they weren't talking...at least about that.

"Tire's plugged," said Tinker.

"Thanks." Gabe paid the man, loaded the tire in the back of his truck, and, once Jessi was settled in the cab, walked back to the office of the station to get, she assumed, the promised map. Minutes later, map in hand, Gabe got in the truck, started the vehicle and drove it onto the highway. Neely Bend soon disappeared behind them.

Jessi sat near the window on the passenger side again since Gabe hadn't invited her to move closer. A glance in his direction found him lost in thought. She could guess why.

"Would you call *that* fate?" Jessi asked.

"Actually, I'd call it humoring the tourists."

"You mean you think he made up that stuff about his gramps?"

"It is mighty coincidental...though he did mark a spot on the map he gave me." Gabe shrugged his bemusement.

"May I see that map?"

"Sure." He tried to hand it to her.

Jessi shook her head. She didn't really want to see the map, she wanted to know what had been whispered to Gabe. Clearly it wasn't anything to do with the location of some mystery ridge. "So what secret did Tinker tell you?"

Gabe gave her a blank look. "Secret...? Oh that. He said the Panther Ridge he knew about was in the middle of nowhere and very hard to get to. He didn't think a woman like you would ever make it, even on an ATV.''

"A woman like—!" Jessi snorted her outrage. "Of all the sexist remarks!"

Gabe burst out laughing. "I don't think women's lib has found Neely Bend, Jessi."

"Oh yeah? And what makes you think that?"

"The fact that ol' Tinker, back there, referred to you as a pretty little filly."

Chapter Seven

"Gabe, look!"

He did, and, for the second time that day, nearly ran off the road. Shaking his head in disgust, Gabe imagined what a mess they'd be in if his truck wound up at the bottom of a ravine along this particularly treacherous and deserted stretch of highway, halfway between Neely Bend and their camp.

"Did you see it?" Jessi demanded, pointing out her window with her right hand, while clutching his arm with her left.

"See what?" he asked, craning to see past her. The terrain on the passenger side of the vehicle sloped downward as sharply as it jutted upward on his side, making it difficult to see anything, at least from his point of view.

"That deer."

Gabe shook his head and concentrated once more on the curving road that some hardworking men and machines had carved into the side of the mountain many years ago. "Missed it, but I saw ten others this morning."

Jessi turned wide eyes on him. "Honestly?"

"At least that many," he told her, no lie. He and August had seen countless deer, not to mention other wildlife, each day they had explored.

"Did you take any pictures?"

"Nah. I was too busy trying to keep up with the boss."

"I thought you were the guide."

"I may be the guide," Gabe answered. "But he's in charge and likes to lead."

"No wonder you needed a hug." Jessi, her gaze now on him, patted his thigh and offered a sympathetic smile.

Gabe cherished her touch and her expression, both of which signaled dawning comprehension of what he'd been through while exploring with August Taylor. Not one to gripe and moan about a demanding "customer"—they were a fact of life, after all—Gabe nonetheless appreciated Jessi's understanding of the patience required to deal with a man who had to have every single thing his way. He wondered if her savvy resulted from being married to a man as bossy.

"Look at all those flowers," his passenger next murmured, her attention once again on the breathtaking scenery. "What are they? Do you know?"

Letting her distract him from his thoughts, Gabe played it safe by edging the truck onto a wide spot on the shoulder and braking so both of them could get a better look. He unfastened his seat belt, then slid over some so he could peer out the window. On the floor of the forest spreading before them, nestled at the feet of tall trees, he spied familiar patches of vibrant color.

"The yellow flowers are probably pale mountain dandelions—it's hard to tell from here—and the purple ones are heal-all."

"Heal-all." Jessi said the words as if trying them on for size. "And what about those red ones, there?" This time she pointed out his window to some bright red flowers that seemed to be growing right out of the rock.

"Hummingbird trumpets." Long fascinated with Mother

Nature's many varieties of wildflowers, Gabe had made it his business to learn the names of as many as possible.

Jessi looked properly impressed by his knowledge and tried out that flower's name, too.

"Hummingbird trumpets." She grinned. "I like that."

"Like most bright-red, tubular flowers, they're pollinated by hummingbirds, which is where they get their name, I guess."

"Makes sense. Now tell me about heal-all, as in does it really?"

Gabe laughed. "Actually, it has been used for years to clean open wounds. How effective it is, I don't know."

"Hmm." She gazed thoughtfully out the window. "Do we have time to climb down there and pick some of the heal-all?"

"Are you wounded?"

Keeping her gaze out the window, Jessi shook her head. "Not yet, but you never know."

No, you don't, Gabe silently agreed and wondered briefly if heal-all worked on battered hearts. "We've got time."

"Will the truck be okay?"

"I'm off the road, and the tire is locked up in back. Besides, we won't go far."

"Thanks, Gabe." From the glove box, Jessi retrieved some napkins she'd put there when they bought Anna Kate an ice cream cone during their first trip together. She then opened the truck door only to shut it again. "I'd better get out on your side," she told him. "It's a little close on mine."

With a nod, Gabe slid over and got out of the truck, then waited while she did the same. After locking the door and pocketing the keys, he led the way to where the flowers grew.

It wasn't an easy walk. The terrain, strewn with leaves and rocks, sloped sharply downward, making each step tricky. Gabe took his time, turning often to help Jessi, whose smooth-soled tennis shoes weren't really appropriate for such a hike.

They reached their destination about ten minutes later, and Jessi immediately stooped over and began to gather the flowers. Though Gabe couldn't really imagine what she wanted with the plants, he didn't complain. It was enough to just watch her toss her hair back over her shoulder so she could see to pick the fragile purple blooms.

Utter peace settled over Gabe, and he sighed, knowing what to thank—the trees, the clear blue sky, the rocks, the flowers, even the bee zipping past his face. He wished he could freeze the moment—save it forever—so that when life got too crazy he could simply pull out this pleasure and relive it.

"What's that noise?"

At Jessi's question, Gabe tuned back in to the present. "Water."

She straightened up, flexing her back as if the bending over weren't doing it any favors. "A creek?"

"More likely a waterfall."

"Where?" she asked, peering down into the shadow-patched woods.

"It's hard to say." Gabe shrugged. "If it's a big fall, then we're a long way from it. If it's small, we're not far at all."

"If we go look for it, will we get lost?"

"You're with the best damn wilderness guide in three states, Jessi. We won't get lost."

"Then do you mind…?" She gave him a smile of apology even as her eyes twinkled with anticipation. "I really haven't been brave enough to explore much, and I'd love to see a natural waterfall."

"I don't mind, but you know you're not dressed for it." He perused her clothing with a critical eye: peach-colored knit pants and matching, oversized sweater plus the tennis shoes. She looked more ready for a shopping trip.

"I'll be okay," she assured him, hastily folding the napkin around the fragile blooms she held.

When Gabe realized she had no pocket and his would harm the flowers, he took off his hat, tucked the napkin in the top of it, and then put the hat back on.

"You're going to need both hands free," he explained, words of wisdom that earned him a nod of agreement from Jessi.

Gabe led the way deeper into the woods, letting more than just the low roar of rushing water guide him. As always when in unfamiliar territory, he relied on his senses. Gabe's ears noted each new sound, and his eyes alerted him to subtle changes in the undergrowth that signaled the presence of moisture. His nose caught the musty scent of wet earth; his skin noticed a new coolness in the air.

As for Gabe's sense of taste…that went untested at the moment, much to his dismay. There was nothing he'd have liked better than to use that particular sense to taste the lips of the woman scrambling down the hillside behind him.

Her soft *oomphs* demonstrated clearly that she was out of her depth here in the wild, but she never slowed or asked for help even though she slipped in the mud and bumped into him from behind more than once.

A glance back revealed the truck could no longer be seen due to the slope of the ground. Gabe smiled encouragement to Jessi, who smiled back. He noted how she held onto the trees as she scrambled past, but he didn't offer assistance. Clearly, she was enjoying this little adventure. He suspected that the difficulty made it that much more fun to her.

"It's really loud now," Jessi commented rather breathlessly several yards further down the path. Loose rocks, disturbed by her steps, rolled past Gabe and then dropped out of sight.

"So loud that I can't understand why we can't see it," Gabe replied, frowning at the tangle of brambles marking the spot where the rocks had vanished. His experience as a guide alerted him to danger; his distraction with Jessi dulled the warning. He took two more steps and then, with a yelp of surprise, stumbled to a halt and threw out an arm to stop Jessi, too.

She crashed into him a second later. "Wha—?"

"Look."

Jessi did and gasped.

A deep ravine yawned right below them. Hidden by the terrain and the undergrowth, it was sweet surprise—a miniparadise. A good-sized waterfall tumbled into a pool as turquoise as the stone in the silver, Indian-crafted ring Gabe had worn on his right hand for years. The rocks that formed the backdrop for the fall and then encircled it sparkled in the afternoon sun. A shimmering rainbow arched the pool. Lush ferns hung over it. Gabe marveled that such a place could stay so well hidden.

"This must be heaven," Jessi murmured with a lusty sigh.

Gabe almost laughed, but then caught sight of her serious expression. She meant what she said, he realized. A veteran of the woods and of other pockets of beauty as awesome at this one, Gabe tried to remember what he felt like the first time he stumbled onto such a place. It wasn't that easy.

Any man became jaded by time and experience. But seeing this particular bit of heaven through Jessi's innocent eyes, sharing her unbridled emotion, helped. Suddenly sheer joy filled him, beginning in the region of his heart and spreading outward until every part of Gabe felt renewed.

Could she change the rest of his world, too? he mused, eyeing her in wonder. Could old hurts be erased and replaced by new, happier experiences? Something told him that was possible. Too bad she wasn't his to keep.

"Why are you looking at me like that?" Jessi demanded. "What's wrong?"

Gabe blinked at his temporary wife and fumbled through

his brain for an answer that wouldn't send her flying back to the truck. "I...uh..."

"Are you all right?" She looked really worried now and clutched his arm.

"I'm fine. Just...overwhelmed."

"Oh." She smiled at him as if in perfect understanding. "I'd think sights like this would be old hat to you."

"Never," he murmured, his gaze on her sweet face, her beautiful body.

Clearly sensing he wasn't talking about the waterfall, Jessi flushed and looked away. "Can we go down there?"

Somehow Gabe redirected his gaze to the scene below. He made note of the rocky terrain with a practiced eye. "Not unless you're a graduate of the Highland California School of Rock Climbing."

She frowned. "There's a rock climbing school in Highland?"

Gabe shook his head and grinned. "That was a joke, Jessi—my lame way of telling you that only an experienced rock climber could get down there."

"You've never climbed down a cliff?"

"I didn't say that."

"Then you have."

"Yes."

"You couldn't tie a rope around my waist and—"

"Nope."

"But—"

"There's no way, Jessi. It wouldn't be safe. Besides, we don't have a rope."

"Oh." She sighed her disappointment and gazed longingly at the pool below.

"We can sit here for a while if you want. We're not punching a clock, after all."

"What about Anna Kate?"

"You know she'll be fine."

Jessi gave him a thoughtful nod, then began to look around for some place to sit. She spied a dead tree on the ground a few feet away, perhaps the product of a lightning strike, and moved toward it. But when she started to sit, Gabe stopped her.

"That's damp. You'll ruin your clothes."

"I don't mind."

"Sure you do." Stepping between Jessi and the log, he sat, stretched out his legs, and patted his lap. "Sit here."

Jessi gave him a look that could've meant anything. "I really don't think…"

"What are you afraid of?"

"Nothing," she told him with a toss of her hair.

"Then sit."

Jessi did…very gingerly and without giving him her full weight. In her obvious care to avoid sitting anywhere near his privates, she wound up rather close to his knees—not the strongest part of his leg.

Gabe guided her back a bit, then, resisting the urge to put his arms around her, he rested his hands on the log on either side of him. She'd relax in time, he thought.

Neither spoke for the next several minutes. Jessi remained stiff as a statue, her eyes glued to the rushing water. Then Gabe felt her jump.

"Look," she whispered, reaching back to turn his face in the indicated direction.

Dragging his gaze from her red hair, now right under his nose and smelling of baby shampoo, Gabe saw what she'd seen: a fawn. Its mother would not be far off, he realized, quickly locating that attentive parent in the bushes nearby. Silently he pointed out the doe to Jessi, who flashed him a brilliant smile. Her violet eyes sparkled like precious jewels. His heart began a jarring thump.

Oh so carefully—he didn't want to scare her—Gabe put his face in Jessi's hair. Lost in her wonder over the scene below them, she didn't seem to notice when he inhaled deeply the shockingly sexy fragrance or raised a hand to test its texture.

Soft. Silky. Just what he'd expected.

Gently Gabe brushed her hair to one side and revealed her ear and neck. Jessi tensed just a little, but whether as a result of his action or the sudden appearance of a huge buck, he didn't know and, at the moment, didn't care. All he could think about was his need to act on the feelings with which he wrestled at this moment—respect, admiration, desire.

Leaning forward just a little, Gabe brushed his lips over her flesh. Jessi never moved. Encouraged by her lack of response—she was either in a trance or didn't mind what he did—Gabe pressed a kiss to Jessi's ear lobe. She tensed at his touch...tensed and turned her head to look him in the eye.

Gabe said nothing...just gazed back at her. The beat of his heart counted off the seconds of silent, mutual staring. One...two...three...

"What do you want from me, Gabe?"

Of all the questions he'd expected, this was not one, so Gabe didn't have a ready answer.

"Another hug?" he finally blurted half-hopefully. This close, this private, she might not give comfort as willingly as she had in the truck. But Jessi turned her body enough that she almost faced him, and slipping her arms under Gabe's, hugged him hard.

"How's this?" she asked, her words muffled against his neck.

"Good," he breathed. "So good."

His heart ticked off several more seconds, then Jessi raised her head to look him in the eye again.

"Is that all you wanted?"

Gabe shook his head.

"What else, then?"

"A kiss?"

Jessi didn't even hesitate, but touched her lips to his. It was the softest of contact, incredibly sensual and, to Gabe, highly erotic. His heart stopped, then began to hammer erratically.

"Ah, Jessi," he murmured against her mouth. "What are you doing to me?"

"Only what you asked me to do," she answered, trailing her kiss over his jawline. That ad-libbed action belied her words and made him shiver violently. Her eyes twinkled in response to his reaction. Gabe groaned and, burying his face against her neck, hugged her so hard she gasped for breath.

"I could get used to having you around."

"Ditto for me," she answered even as she wedged her hands between their bodies and gave him a gentle push away. "But we mustn't."

"Why not?"

"Our dreams don't match."

"So we'll change them." At that moment Gabe actually believed that to be possible, and, intoxicated by Jessi's nearness, didn't have sense enough to question his belief.

"*We* will? You mean you'd give up your Snake River plans?" Her gaze searched his face.

As effective as a bucket of ice water, her astute question sobered Gabe. "No...I mean, I..." He shook his head and gave her a smile of apology. "I don't know what I was thinking," he murmured, even as she stood. He did the same. "Must've been this—" he indicated the beauty around them "—getting to me." His gazed locked with Jessi's. "Or, more likely, it was you...every man's dream wife."

Jessi laughed as if he'd just said the craziest thing in the world, a sound that startled the deer. They bounded into the woods with a crash of limbs, leaving Gabe and Jessi as alone as two people could be in a forest full of curious insects and watchful wildlife.

"Believe me, Gabe, I'm no dream wife. In fact, according to my ex, I spend too much time in the kitchen—"

"Impossible."

"Clean too much."

"No such thing."

"And I'm lousy in bed."

It was Gabe's turn to laugh. "Lady, you must've been married to an idiot...or maybe, maybe he was just selfish. Maybe he didn't know how much better it would be if he took his time, looked, listened, and experimented...."

"Don't..." She looked away, visibly affected by his words.

The sound of her ragged breaths was music to Gabe's ears. "Believe me, it wasn't you, Jessi. I promise that. You're an incredibly responsive woman. You set me on fire, and if the time were right, I know I could make you feel the same."

"I know it too. In fact, you have already."

Her softly uttered words struck him like a blow to the back of his knees. And, decidedly off balance, Gabe leaned against a nearby tree to keep from falling down.

"Come 'ere," he murmured, reaching out for Jessi.

She came to him, slipping into his embrace and nestling her body against his as if she needed the comfort this time, as if she belonged there. Gabe believed she did...at least at that moment. He refused to think beyond the time they would leave this paradise on earth.

Tenderly, testing, he kissed her. Jessi kissed him back, at first tentatively, then with more enthusiasm. Once Gabe felt her willing cooperation in the effort, he deepened the contact by touching his tongue to her lips, which she immediately parted for him. He treasured her willingness, knowing she had doubts about him and even herself. He savored the taste of her, just as she seemed to savor the taste of him.

In fact, every move he made, she copied until their tongues mated and his heart rate skyrocketed. Shockingly weak in the knees, Gabe used the tree behind him as a guide to safer ground, sliding down until his backside made contact with moss-covered earth. Jessi went with him, landing on her knees between his thighs. No longer at eye level, they had to break the kiss, but Gabe didn't mind. There was more of Jessi to learn, beginning with the part of her at eye level now.

Wrapping his arms around Jessi's hips, Gabe buried his face in her sweater, breast high. When she pressed her palms to the tree trunk over his head and leaned even closer, he slipped one hand under her clothing and traced the curves he found there.

So full. So sexy.

It was almost too much for him, and with a soft groan, Gabe tipped his head back and closed his eyes.

"Are you taking a nap?" Jessi asked.

Gabe gave her an incredulous look. "Are you kidding?"

"Yeah," she told him, laughing softly. "Yeah, I am." He noted a new confidence in her demeanor, a playfulness, and liked it.

In one swift move, Gabe pulled Jessi to him and took them both down to the ground. That put Jessi full on top of him, a position she quickly altered by straddling his waist.

Highly aware of her backside pressed to his bulging fly, Gabe slipped both hands under Jessi's sweater this time and palmed her lace-encased breasts. She caught her breath and, lowering her face, kissed his cheek, his eyes, his nose. Gabe responded by slipping his arms around her back and pulling her down tightly against him. Somehow her kiss found his mouth, and as her lips moved over his, Gabe unfastened her bra, then let his hands explore her back, hips and bare breasts.

Damn, but she felt good to the touch. He wanted to make love to her. No, he wanted to make love *with* her. Gabe knew the difference, as Jessi's ex apparently had not.

At that moment, Jessi raised up and smiled at him. Her hair, falling just any which way around her face, shone almost copper in the golden glow of the sinking sun.

Sinking sun?

Surely not.

Taking care to hide the movement, Gabe tried to get a

look at his watch. He didn't think Jessi noticed the action...until she caught his wrist in her hand.

"My God! Is that really the time?" she exclaimed.

"Who cares?" Gabe asked even as he realized that what he had in mind for him and Jessi would take much more time than was left in this day.

"Apparently you do. Why else would you look at your watch?" she demanded, scrambling off him and refastening her bra. Clearly she thought him bored with their lovemaking.

"Jessi, I—"

"You don't have to explain, Gabe." She turned away then, and moved toward the trail they had forged down the mountainside on their climb down.

"Oh, yes, I do," he answered, grabbing her arm, yanking her back into his embrace. Capturing her chin in his hand, Gabe stole a kiss—stole it because Jessi didn't cooperate.

At first, anyway. Determined that she would realize the effect she had on him, Gabe put his heart and soul into the contact, and in seconds, she clung to him as if *her* knees had suffered a crippling blow.

"I want you more than anything," Gabe murmured once the kiss ended and she sagged against him. "But I don't want to rush."

"It's hours until dark," Jessi answered, glancing up at the sky.

"And hours are what I need."

She looked at him in disbelief. "Hours...?"

"Hours...days...months...even years might not be enough."

Jessi's wide-eyed gaze swallowed him whole. "What are you saying to me, Gabe?"

"I'm saying...I'm saying..." He gulped audibly. "Hell, I don't know what I'm saying."

"That sounded like a proposal."

Gabe shook his head. "It wasn't."

"What was it then? A proposition?" She looked hurt, almost angry.

"Not that either."

"Then what?"

"I told you I don't know!" Running his hands through his hair, badly in need of a cut, Gabe snatched up his hat and sat it on his head. "I'm not myself right now, okay? I'm aroused. I'm confused. I'm—"

"Leaving?"

Gabe hesitated, then glanced in the direction the truck was parked and nodded. "That's right. I'm leaving, and so are you. And when we're someplace different, someplace that isn't so—"

"Romantic?" Her tone was sarcastic.

"—we'll have a real heart-to-heart talk and sort this thing out." He clasped her by the shoulders. His gazed locked with hers. "Okay?"

"Okay," Jessi answered, adding almost sadly, "And I can predict we won't feel the same."

"Oh, I think we will," Gabe answered, tactfully not adding that the idea scared him half to death.

"Yeah? And what makes you so sure?"

"Because I believe it isn't just the location that's making us so crazy this afternoon. I believe it's—"

"This man?" She sounded almost tender now, and traced his jawline with her finger.

Gabe shook his head and captured her hand in his so he could kiss that precious finger. "No. It's the woman, Jessi. Like I said before...it's you."

Chapter Eight

Jessi hadn't been back in the truck ten minutes before the gravity of their foolishness hit home. She stole a glance at Gabe and found him pensive—no surprise. He surely had second thoughts, too. Theirs was a momentary marriage, after all. They barely knew each other, had little in common, and dreamed different dreams. She'd said as much herself, then lay with him in the woods like some wanton wild woman.

Glancing down at her clothes, Jessi made a belated inspection to see if she'd brought any of that woods into the truck with her. Not surprisingly, she found her sweater littered with bits of leaf and grass. Then there was the matter of her pants, the knees of which she found streaked with grass stain.

With a huff of disgust, Jessi began to brush herself off.

"Are they ruined?" Gabe asked, eyeing her peach pants.

"I doubt it. They're just cotton and usually wash well." Jessi inspected his shirt. "Remind me to brush you off the minute we get to camp. We don't want August and Shari thinking we've been rolling in the leaves together."

"It would be all right if we had been," Gabe said. "In fact, it might even be good if they assume we stopped along the way for a little hanky-panky. We are married, you know. It would only be natural for us to take advantage of being alone."

Jessi said nothing to that. Though true, his words disturbed since they reminded her of a near miss she wanted desperately to forget. Thank goodness for Anna Kate. That precious moppet was all that would save Jessi from the heart-to-heart Gabe had promised back in the woods. Suspecting that he was right, that they might find their attraction was more than the by-product of a secluded, romantic setting, Jessi vowed right then to keep her daughter close at hand for the rest of their adventure.

If Jessi and Gabe had more than sexual curiosity between them, Jessi just didn't want to know.

Not that sexual curiosity wasn't problem enough. It definitely was. Worse, Gabriel had undoubtedly figured out that she couldn't resist him. Men just seemed to sense those things, and, when they did, invariably used the knowledge. Having confessed to a less-than-satisfying sexual experience with her ex, Jessi suspected that she especially challenged Gabe. Why, he probably couldn't wait to get his hands on her again to see if he could kiss her into submission.

Unfortunately, Jessi knew that he could, and that it wouldn't take long. Why, they'd almost reached such a point in the woods.

Shuddering at the thought, she reminded herself that Gabe had plans for his life, noble plans that included adopting his ten-year-old nephew. Thank goodness he didn't have time for the challenge of one Jessi Landers, even if she could be tempted to abandon her own plans.

But what if he found time? What then?

Jessi knew exactly what then. She'd put her own dreams on hold and link her life with his for as long as he'd have her. Idiot, she chided herself. Had her bad marriage taught her nothing about the perils of living for a man? And what about all her big plans to get out of debt, start a business, finally be her own boss?

Depressed by the knowledge that Gabe could so quickly scramble her goals, Jessi settled into a funk that lasted long after they returned to camp. Even Anna Kate's delight with her teddy bear did not lift Jessi's spirits, and neither did the successful retrieval of the abandoned ATV.

It came as no surprise when August later announced that they would pack up camp the next day and head north seeking the Panther Ridge that Tinker, the garage owner, had talked about. Tonight August appeared especially restless, perhaps a little desperate...or were her own feelings tinting her outlook?

They agreed that they would pack up after dinner that night so they could hit the road early the next day. Jessi chose hot dogs for the evening meal and charged Anna Kate and Gabe with gathering wood for the fire.

Just an hour after their arrival at camp, Jessi and Gabe sat around the crackling flames with August, Shari and Anna Kate. Jessi had traded her peach pants for jeans since she couldn't bear the reminder of what she'd let Gabe do to her in the woods. Besides that, she didn't want her employers wondering about the grass stain.

Not that they hadn't believed Jessi's spur-of-the moment explanation about picking wildflowers. They had—or at least seemed to—and examined the heal-all she'd picked. But as long as Jessi wore those pants, she would feel like a teenaged girl caught doing grown-up things with a teenaged boy in the back seat of his dad's car.

Dessert consisted of a campout favorite—s'mores. Using ingredients bought in Neely Bend, Jessi stacked graham crackers, chocolate bars and marshmallows, then roasted them over the fire. The delicious results completed a good out-of-doors meal, and Jessi felt a pang of disappointment that they would leave this beautiful campsite the next day.

During pack-up, which by now they'd reduced to an art,

it began to sprinkle rain. By bedtime, the heavens let loose with a torrential downpour. And though Jessi hadn't expected to sleep a wink that night, the sound of the rain pattering steadily on their metal roof lulled her right into a deep, dreamless slumber.

She woke to light drizzle on Thursday, feeling slightly drugged instead of refreshed. After a quick breakfast of bacon-and-egg sandwiches, the men pulled their fully-loaded trucks and campers onto the highway to begin the two-hour drive to a new location.

By then, Jessi nursed a throbbing headache. Anna Kate, however, felt great, as evidenced by her constant chatter and singing. Gabe appeared to be in good spirits too, which was lucky. He and Anna Kate tossed around possible names for the bear, then Gabe kept the girl entertained with stories both improvised and true. Jessi just stared out the window.

When they passed the spot where Gabe had parked the truck the day before, Jessi caught his eye. The look he gave her really could, as Shari had pointed out, "melt steel," and she quickly turned her head to avoid the heat. Had the man no remorse? Didn't he realize the folly of what they'd done?

Now she couldn't look at his face without remembering the scrape of his five o'clock shadow, the contrasting smoothness of his lips. The sight of his hands, gripping the steering wheel, reminded her of his touch, and the tips of her breasts actually hardened as if he had those hands on them now. As for his long legs, she well recalled their strength and the feel of being pinned between them.

Damn, but she wished they'd completed what they started yesterday. With luck he'd have been a lousy lover easily forgotten...but no. The sensations he evoked in her already proved that an impossibility. Gabe would be good—very, very good. And just thinking about lying on top of him in the woods made her body ache in the most secret of places.

The men made one planned stop to buy ice and replenish

their water supply while en route to their new camp, and one unplanned stop to accommodate Anna Kate, who'd downed a cola. Nonetheless, they made good time to their destination, and then got lucky in that they found the perfect place to set up camp.

Or not so perfect, Jessi decided moments after she and Gabe unhooked the camper and began to level it. This camp, she realized, was a far more rugged area than their first location, with tangled undergrowth, towering hardwoods, and some downed pines that reminded her this was logging country.

"Are you sure we're not trespassing on someone's private property?" she asked Gabe.

"Not according to the map," he answered. "But if someone complains, we'll move. Meanwhile, we're all dedicated to leaving camp just the way we found it, so when we pull out tomorrow, no one is even going to know we were here."

"Tomorrow? You mean you honestly think our Panther Ridge is around here?"

Abandoning the hydraulic lift he manipulated, Gabe stood, stepped behind Jessi and turned her to face another direction.

"See that rock formation right there?"

Jessi nodded.

"What does it look like?"

She considered the high-rising formation for several seconds from several angles, then caught her breath. "A panther's head."

"Bingo." Gabe wrapped his arms around her middle and rested his chin on the top of her head. "This may be it, babe."

Babe? Jessi's heart kicked into overdrive. She could barely breathe.

"Gabe, we need to talk." Jessi struggled with every word.

"Later, okay? August is champing at the bit, and I want

to get this camper leveled before we leave." He stepped back and grinned at her. "If I don't, you won't be able to cook, and that, madam chef, would be a tragedy since my breakfast sandwich is lo-o-ng gone."

"Oh gosh!" Jessi blurted, whirling to face him. "I've got to pack you guys a lunch."

Gabe nodded, then laughed when she darted for the camper door. "Wait! Let me finish up here."

Jessi nodded and glanced around for Anna Kate. She found her daughter sitting on the ground near a stump, which the girl apparently used for a table. Anna Kate's miniature china tea set already dotted the top of it, and her dolly and still-nameless teddy bear now waited to be served.

Thank goodness the child could be trusted to entertain herself, Jessi thought even as Gabe waved her on into the camper. Once there, she made short work of preparing ham sandwiches for the men—two apiece. Jessi threw in fresh fruit, chips and cookies, then exited the camper to find August and Gabe aboard their ATV's and waiting for her.

She handed Gabe the insulated lunch bag and took one step back, only to be captured by his right arm and pulled close again.

"See you later, Jessi," he said loud enough for everyone to hear. Much softer, he added, "And we'll have that talk." Then he kissed her—a kiss to end all kisses that involved lips, teeth and tongues and left her gasping for air.

That bold gesture earned Jessi a knowing look from Shari as well as a giggle from Anna Kate, who appeared downright smug and definitely pleased. Struggling to get her wits together again, Jessi waved to her husband, then slipped inside the camper, where she splashed cold water on her face. Long after silence settled on the camp, Jessi still hid in her temporary home, busying herself with nothing in particular.

A soft knock drew her to the door. There she found Shari and Anna Kate.

"Are you okay?" Shari asked, clearly concerned. "A.K. said you have a headache."

"A.K.?"

"That's my new name!" Anna Kate exclaimed, beaming. "A is for Anna. K is for Kate. Shari told me."

Jessi had to laugh, and actually felt a bit better. "Well, at least you'll know two letters when you start first grade."

"But I know 'em all," her daughter argued and then sang the alphabet song to prove it. Jessi winced at the enthusiastic rendition, which fairly shook the windows. So much for coddling her headache. With this rambunctious four-year-old around, there was no such luxury.

Particularly pleased to have that child there, Jessi caught up her daughter in a hug and planted a noisy kiss on the top of her head. Anna Kate—or A.K. as she obviously wanted to be called—hugged her mom back with abandon.

"Want some coffee or cocoa?" Shari asked.

"Cocoa sounds great to me," Jessi answered, releasing her daughter.

"Me too!" the girl chimed in.

Though Jessi moved toward the stove to help, Shari waved her away. "You pamper that head of yours," she said, adding, "Have you taken anything for it?"

"No," Jessi admitted.

"Got anything?" Shari asked.

"Heal-all?"

Shari laughed at that. "Somehow I think aspirin might be better."

"Right," Jessi murmured, heading to the first aid box and helping herself to a couple of tablets. She put the aspirin back on the top shelf, out of reach of her daughter.

The women sat in the eating booth and sipped hot chocolate for the next half hour. They talked about anything and everything, a great distraction for Jessi, who suddenly realized her head felt somewhat better.

"You know," Shari murmured. "It would be easy to

lose track of time out here. I mean the days just seem to blur, don't they?''

"Yes, they do," Jessi answered. "In fact, I'm not even sure what day it is…Tuesday…Wednesday?''

"Thursday, October 20th.''

Jessi laughed out loud at that bit of news. "My birthday!''

"Are you serious?" asked Shari.

Jessi nodded. "First birthday I've ever totally forgotten, by the way.''

"Let's have a party," Shari suggested. "Want to?''

Anna Kate squealed her delight with the idea, clapping her hands and dancing around the trailer. "A birthday party! We're going to have a birthday party!''

"A wonderful birthday party," Shari amended, eyes sparkling.

She looked as excited at Anna Kate, so Jessi swallowed back her immediate protest.

"I'll do everything…even bake the cake." The next instant, Shari grinned somewhat sheepishly at Jessi. "Not that I've ever baked one before, mind you, but if you'll sit right where you are and tell me everything to do, I'm sure I can manage. Will you help me, please?''

"Please?" Anna Kate added her entreaty to Shari's.

How could Jessi refuse them? "Oh, all right, but I'm not sure turning thirty-one is anything to celebrate.''

"Why, that's young yet," Shari argued. Jessi guessed she could afford to be generous since she probably wasn't anywhere near that old herself. "In fact, I read about some movie star in her fifties who just had twins.''

"Heaven help her," Jessi murmured from the heart, an answer that made Shari laugh.

"Well, you might not want to wait that long before you and Gabe have children, but there is still plenty of time…or is that even what's bothering you?''

Anna Kate spun around and charged the table. "Are you gonna have a baby?''

"No," Jessi quickly assured her.

"Why not?"

Because I haven't had sex in a zillion years, Jessi wanted to reply. She didn't of course. "I have you. I don't need a baby."

"But I want a little sister like Heather."

And I want a water bed like her mom, not to mention a man to go in it. "You'll have to settle for a big brother, I'm afraid," Jessi answered, the next second nearly falling off the bench. Had she honestly said that? Referred to Ryder as if he were going to be part of her family instead of Gabe's? Jessi gave herself a mental kick in the backside and glanced worriedly toward Anna Kate.

"Ryder?" the child predictably asked.

"Who's Ryder?" Shari asked before Jessi could think of an answer.

"Gabe's nephew." Jessi casually sipped her chocolate and tried to look relaxed.

"He's gonna a-dopt him," Anna Kate said, carefully pronouncing her new word.

"How old is Ryder?" Clearly, Shari had questions.

"Ten." Evidently, Anna Kate, now playing with her bear on the floor, had answers.

Shari took advantage of that. "Where is he now?"

Anna Kate glanced at her mother for help.

"Los Angeles. Ryder is the son of Gabe's sister, who died recently. Gabe plans to adopt him as soon as he can afford to, one of the reasons he was so excited about August's job offer, which was very generous and should help Gabe—er, *us*—get his new business started and pay a lawyer."

"Tell me about this new business."

Jessi did, using Gabe's own words to describe the venture.

"You'll manage the café, of course."

Jessi smiled in answer to keep from lying.

"I bet you'll love it."

I probably would, Jessi realized, toying for just a second with the idea of investing in Gabe's Snake River enterprise. Would he let her? she wondered even as Shari spoke again and scattered Jessi's thoughts.

"I guess you two would've done anything to get this job...." Shari looked thoughtful.

Jessi, who considered this conversation very hazardous, shrugged and glanced at her daughter, who thankfully didn't appear to be listening anymore. "Yes."

"I know that August has made his apology for making you two get married, but I want to add my own. It was just so stupid. My only consolation is that it was just a matter of time before you got around to a wedding anyway." Her eyes pleaded with Jessi to agree.

But Jessi could only stare. "August apologized?"

Shari nodded. "Gabe didn't tell you?"

"No." Jessi mulled over this bit of trivia. "So Gabe and I really didn't have to marry?"

"Well, you did *then*, but wouldn't have now." Shari frowned. "I hope you aren't upset. I couldn't stand it if you were."

"I'm not upset...at least not with August. I am a little irritated about not being told he'd changed his mind."

"I guess Gabe forgot in all the excitement of meeting, getting to know each other, and—"

"You mean he's known since the beginning?"

Shari nodded. "Is something wrong? Are you angry?"

"No to both," Jessi lied, faking a smile. "This just changes my view of August, and I wish I'd known sooner."

"He's really not so bad," Shari murmured, no doubt assuming that Jessi now felt guilty about disliking her husband.

Jessi reached across the table and grasped Shari's hand. "I never thought he was bad, exactly, just a little interfering."

Shari sighed. "You're so right, and I apologize again for

him. Now please tell me my meddling husband didn't ruin your life by demanding a wedding.''

"Of course not.''

"And you forgive him?''

"I do. I really like August, Shari. He's a good man.''

"Yes, he is,'' Shari said, swiping at the tears that had pooled in her eyes and now rolled down her cheek.

"What's wrong with Shari?'' demanded Anna Kate from her spot near the love seat.

"It's a woman thing,'' Jessi told her.

"I'm a woman,'' Anna Kate answered, leaping to her feet. She threw out her chest, tossed her hair and strutted as though to prove it, actions no doubt copied from her idol, Miss Piggy.

Jessi and Shari both laughed. "Not yet, thank goodness, but you are old enough to help Shari with my cake...that is if she still wants to make it.''

"Oh, I do!'' Shari slid out of the eating booth and walked over to the pantry. "Now what do I need?''

"A recipe, for starters,'' Jessi told her, setting in motion what turned out to be an entertaining afternoon in the kitchen. Only when Shari began to read and follow the recipe they'd selected, about fifteen minutes later, did Jessi allow herself to analyze Gabe's motives for keeping August's apology a secret.

She could think of none for that or for the fact that Gabe had also maintained the secret of their true relationship even though it no longer mattered to August. Then she began to wonder if it was because Gabe actually liked being married or—her heart suddenly beat a little faster—had fallen for her.

But no. They'd only just met at that time. So his reason had to be simpler.

Maybe he likes the fringe benefits.

Remembering yesterday's conversation about hanky-panky and today's shocker of a kiss, Jessi feared that theory was the right one.

"This table turns into a bed," Anna Kate suddenly announced, breaking into Jessi's musings.

"I know," Shari answered. "Do you like it?"

"I don't sleep here. Gabe does."

"*He does?*" Shari turned wide, questioning eyes to Jessi, who felt her face begin to burn.

"I have a great idea!" Jessi exclaimed, leaping to her feet and grabbing Anna Kate by the wrist. "Why don't the two of us go outside and pick some wildflowers for the cake?"

"But it's raining," argued her daughter.

"We won't melt," Jessi retorted, as good as dragging the girl out the door.

Somehow Jessi avoided being totally alone with Shari the entire day. She did intercept more than one puzzled stare and wished to high heaven that Anna Kate had just kept her mouth shut about the beds.

Children and their honesty...man, oh man.

Dusk settled over camp before the men returned. Both women, anxious by then, ran out into the sprinkling rain to meet them.

"Any luck?" Shari blurted just a millisecond before both she and Jessi spotted two strongboxes of rusted metal, strapped with bungee cord to the rear rack. "Is this it? Is this the gold?" Wide-eyed and clearly thrilled, she ran her hands over the box, which wasn't much larger than a shoebox.

"No gold."

That clipped answer came from August, who dismounted his ATV and began to unload his share of the paraphernalia the men considered necessary to this treasure hunt. He left the box for Shari to unload, sure indication that there wasn't anything of weight or worth in it, either.

Gabe, now standing by his own ATV, caught Jessi's questioning look and just shook his head. She noted that he seemed much less disappointed, an interesting reaction to say the least. Her own spirits plummeted.

Without a word, he handed her the empty lunch bag, then turned to unload the second strongbox, which was identical to the first, followed by his gun and the camera equipment. By then, Anna Kate had abandoned her television and rushed outside to join them.

"Treasure!" she cried. "You found treasure!"

"Not exactly," Gabe quickly responded, reaching out to tug Anna Kate's ponytail.

"You mean no money?"

"Nope."

"No diamonds?"

"Nope."

"No pearls?"

"No nothing worth anything," August growled, putting a no-more-nonsense end to Anna Kate's persistent questioning.

Clearly unperturbed by his gruff response, Anna Kate danced around her mother, who still held one of the boxes. "Can I see inside it? Can I?"

"In a minute," Jessi answered with a worried glance toward August. Visibly grim, the writer turned and headed toward his trailer.

Shari took the strongbox from their ATV and handed it to Anna Kate. "We'll be over for the party in a few minutes," the blonde promised in a low voice before following her husband into their trailer.

Doubting the wisdom of any kind of celebration tonight, Jessi glanced at Gabe to see his reaction to Shari's words. But he had already walked halfway to their trailer, where he stood slipping off his rain poncho as if he hadn't heard. At any rate he made no comment, until he stepped into the kitchen and saw the decorated cake.

"What's the occa—" he began, breaking off to turn and look back at Jessi and Anna Kate, now standing just outside the trailer door. "Aww man. It's your birthday, isn't it, Jessi?"

She and Anna Kate both nodded.

"Well shoot," Gabe muttered, taking off his hat and tossing it to the love seat. He set down the rest of his things, too, every movement silent proclamation of his disgust about something. Jessi guessed what, and so, apparently, did her daughter.

"You forgot, didn't you?" Anna Kate accused, setting her box down on the table and shaking a finger at her Daddy G.

"I sure did, honey," Gabe replied with a sigh.

"It doesn't matter," Jessi hastily assured him, putting her box next to Anna Kate's. "I actually forgot it myself."

"It does matter, too." He heaved a sigh and finger combed his shaggy hair back off his forehead. "I'm sorry, Jessi."

"It's okay. Really."

"Me and Shari made her something," Anna Kate told Gabe, words that didn't seem to comfort him.

"Oh yeah?" Gabe sat on the edge of one of the eating booth's bench seats. "And what did you two make?"

"It's a secret, silly," Anna Kate replied, the next second glancing over at her mother, who gave her an I'm-gonna-get-you look. Anna Kate climbed right into Gabe's lap and threw her arms around his neck in a choke hold that seemed to answer Jessi back, *you'll have to go through him!*

Jessi, noting Gabe's delight at her daughter's spontaneity, didn't even try, but turned her back on the pair of them and busied herself locating the bowls and spoons needed for tonight's dinner of vegetable soup. She'd figured the men might appreciate the warm-up after a hard day exploring caves. Gabe's immediate look of pleasure told her she hadn't missed the mark.

He and Anna Kate began to whisper shortly afterward and then disappeared into the bedroom, where they stayed until Jessi heard a knock on the door some twenty minutes later. She called out a welcome to August and Shari, who stepped into the trailer just as Gabe and Anna Kate left the bedroom.

"So what was in the boxes?" asked Shari, her tone almost too cheerful.

Guessing that her new friend was trying to make the most of a bad situation, Jessi did her best to help out.

"We were waiting for you to get here so we could open them," Jessi said to Shari and motioned the pair to come in. She cleaned off the built-in love seat so they could sit. Once they got comfortable, she turned to Gabe. "Drumroll, please."

Gabe played the tabletop much as a musician would play bongo drums.

"Anna Kate, will you do the honors?"

Anna Kate certainly would and, with a little assistance from Gabe, did, tossing back the corroded metal lid to reveal the contents inside. When the child reached into the first box, Shari leapt to her feet to get a better look. She and Jessi both watched as Anna Kate removed several photographs, some tattered papers and what looked to be a book of some kind from the box. Feeling oddly let down, Jessi picked up the book and opened it.

"Silas McHenry," she read from inside the front cover before turning and inspecting a few water-stained, handwritten pages. A feeling of awe washed over her. "Another journal." She turned to August. "Will this help you in any way?"

Her employer, who'd certainly examined everything already, just shrugged.

"Surely this is worth something to someone," Jessi murmured, undaunted. "Either as a collectible, a piece of history, a family heirloom...?"

August said nothing.

"Look, Mommy." Anna Kate held out one of the yellowed photographs, which Jessi took and inspected. It was of a young woman holding a baby, perhaps Silas's wife and child. Another featured an older couple. His parents?

"Does the second box have more of the same?" Shari asked. She handed the paper she held to Jessi, who quickly discovered it to be a letter from someone named Rachel.

"Yes," Gabe answered, adding, "The boxes were unlocked when we found them, which means any gold these men found was stolen long ago."

"I'm so sorry," Jessi murmured, glancing first at her husband then at August. Though August still made no response, Gabe gave her a half smile.

"Hey," he murmured. "We've got nine more treasure hunts to go. One, maybe even more of them is bound to pan out. Now I don't know about you folks, but I'm starved. How about some of that soup?" His eyes pleaded with Jessi to move right along.

Carefully replacing the photos, journal and letters in the box, which must have been important to Silas, Jessi did as requested. "Shari, would you mind getting the drinks?"

Shari fixed everyone their beverage of choice while Jessi filled each soup bowl from the large stew pot simmering on the gas stove. That accomplished, she piled a basket high with crackers, then joined her companions, now seated at the table, Gabe on one side, Shari and August on the other. At Anna Kate's insistence, Jessi slipped in the booth beside Gabe. The girl then sat beside her.

The five of them ate in silence for several minutes by the light of a kerosene lamp. When that silence began to feel awkward, Jessi felt compelled to break it.

"Did it rain all day?" she asked, getting up to get the iced tea pitcher.

"Yes," Gabe answered, handing her his glass for a refill. "Thank God for waterproof gear."

"So where do we go next?" Shari asked, her gaze on her silent husband.

"Oregon, I guess." His lack of enthusiasm wasn't lost

on his wife, who lay her arms over his shoulders in a quick hug.

"Gabe's right, you know," Shari said. "This is just our first find."

"Yeah, well the way I feel right now, it might be our last." Nudging Shari to move out of the way, he tried to slip off the bench.

But his beautiful wife didn't cooperate. "You can't leave yet. We're going to have a birthday party."

August didn't even ask whose. "I'm too tired."

"Surely you've got enough energy left to eat a piece of cake." Shari beamed at him. "I made it."

Her husband just shook his head, and obviously taking his hint, Shari silently slipped out of the booth to let him by. Before August could move, Anna Kate leapt off the opposite bench, skirted the table and scrambled up beside him.

"Please stay for the party," she begged. "Please, please, please."

August positively scowled at the four-year-old—an expression that should have sent her scurrying for cover.

Instead, Anna Kate reached out both hands and tried to spread his lips into a smile.

Jessi caught her breath at the precocious action, as did Shari. Gabe just sat very still…almost as if he anticipated defending his stepdaughter's life at any moment.

As for August, he glared at Anna Kate for one second, then another before he gave in and helped with the smile. That reluctant smile turned first into a grin, then a chuckle, a sound that instantly dissolved the tension in the room.

"Did you help Shari with the cake?" August asked.

Anna Kate nodded.

"And is it good?"

"The best," she told him.

"Then I guess I'd better stay and try some. Can't have you two—" belatedly he smiled at Jessi "—make that *three* ladies mad at me."

Chapter Nine

"Best cake I ever ate," August announced a good half hour later after swallowing the last bite of a generous slice. He turned to Shari, still seated next to him. "You really made it?"

"Yes."

"Well, you did a great job." August looked at Anna Kate. "What's next? Pin the tail on the donkey?"

Anna Kate giggled and slid off the bench seat to dispose of her paper plate. "Presents. Cool ones."

"So let's get started," August responded, rubbing his hands together as if excited about the prospect of watching Jessi open her presents, an act that earned him Jessi's gratitude.

At once, Anna Kate reached into the storage bin located under the love seat and pulled out a card and a medium-sized box wrapped in aluminum foil. She handed them to her mother, who'd left the table to throw away her own plate; then Anna Kate added a birthday kiss and an "I love you" so precious that Jessi almost burst into tears.

The card, decorated with crayon drawings, also boasted

a poem that had obviously been written down by Shari, but had surely been composed by Anna Kate herself. While a little short on rhyme, it nonetheless served the purpose, and once again Jessi had to blink back tears.

In the box, Jessi found a necklace made of wildflowers cleverly strung together, lei-like, stem to bloom.

"Why, this is gorgeous!" she exclaimed, slipping it over her head. She turned to Gabe, who now stood near the sink refilling his glass with cola. "What kind of flowers are these?"

He fingered one of the bright yellow blooms. "Tansies. They've been used since ancient times for medicinal purposes, but very carefully since ingestion can prove fatal."

Jessi pointed a finger at her daughter. "Do not eat these."

Anna Kate's expression of utter disbelief told everyone the idea had never crossed her mind.

"Tansies also keep flies away," Gabe added in a teasing tone, adding, "So if you want to skip your bath tonight…"

With a huff of outrage, Jessi swatted at Gabe, who caught her up in his embrace and held her prisoner there. Now standing on tiptoe out of necessity, she blushed and squirmed to be free, but Gabe did not let her go.

"I have a present for you," he said, his mouth mere inches from hers.

"Oh really?" Jessi's heart began to pound in anticipation of a gift that was surely not what he intended to give—or maybe it was, she amended, suddenly remembering Shari's revelation that morning and her own questions regarding Gabe's motivation for maintaining their marriage charade.

"You're re-e-ally gonna like it," Anna Kate added, further piquing her mother's curiosity.

"So where is this wonderful present?" Jessi disentangled herself with care. Though Shari had said it no longer mattered if Jessi and Gabe were married, Jessi saw no way to reveal the truth of their relationship without appearing dishonest.

Was this Gabe's reason, also?

"Now I never said it was wonderful," her temporary husband murmured, smiling somewhat sheepishly. From his pocket he withdrew a piece of clear plastic, cut in the shape of a two-inch by two-inch square. Mounted in the center of it, Jessi spied a four-leaf clover.

She raised her gaze to Gabe, questioning him without words for the story behind it.

He shrugged and stuffed his fingertips in the front pocket of his jeans, looking for all the world as if he were shy, something he definitely was not.

"I found it years ago and had it laminated," he told her. "My luck seemed to change that very day. I figure it's time to pass my good fortune along to someone else—" he suddenly tensed and glanced at his employer "—in particular a someone else I'm married to."

"Why, thank you, Gabe," Jessi responded, truly touched.

"And now it's time for my presents," announced Shari with a mischievous laugh that seemed to say something— who knew what?—had amused her. "First is a family photo." Retrieving a Polaroid camera from under the love seat, where it had apparently been stashed earlier, Shari motioned for Gabe, Jessi and Anna Kate to move closer together. She peered through the camera viewfinder at them. "Gabe, you're either too tall or A.K.—"

"A.K.?" questioned both men at the same time.

"*Anna Kate*" replied Shari, "is too small. Why don't you sit on that couch thing there. Jessi can sit next to you. A.K., get in your dad's lap, would you?"

Gabe, Jess and her daughter all did as requested.

"Much better," Shari said after another peek through the camera. "But not perfect. Gabe, put your arm around Jessi's back. Jessi, I want you to put your arms around Gabe's waist and your cheek on his shoulder. A.K., give your dad a kiss."

Again all three obeyed.

"Perfect!" Shari exclaimed just seconds before a bright flash illuminated that corner of the trailer. She pulled the shot from the camera and set both aside. "Now for my other present…and this is where the four-leaf-clover comes in. Tonight is your lucky night, Jessi Dillard. A.K. is sleeping over with August and me, which means you and your husband have this trailer *all to yourselves!*"

"Oh, Shari, you mustn't," blurted Jessi without thought. The next second she tried to cover up her blunder. "It's too much trouble."

"Trouble, nothing. It'll be fun. Why, A.K. and I have looked forward to this surprise all day, haven't we?"

Anna Kate nodded enthusiastically.

"But August—" began Jessi.

"Doesn't mind a bit," interjected her bear of an employer, his features softened by a smile so charming, and so sincere, that Jessi couldn't believe her eyes. "Please cooperate. You and your husband deserve the privacy since we cheated you out of your honeymoon."

Guessing Shari had decided a lack of privacy was the reason Gabe slept alone and so now wanted to help out, Jessi graciously muttered embarrassed appreciation for the gift. Gabe, looking a bit flustered himself, added his thank-you.

Not five minutes later, around ten o'clock, the party abruptly ended, but not before everyone, including August, exclaimed over the photo, which proved to be a delightful family portrait, and, therefore, a disconcerting lie. Jessi barely maintained her smile until the door shut behind her guests, at which point she began to clean up the rest of the party mess to hide an intense discomfort at deceiving her employers, being a year older, and finding herself so alone with her handsome, tempting husband.

Gabe helped her…or tried to. He actually got underfoot more than anything else, and Jessi finally begged him to just sit down and let her do it.

"You know," he said as he obediently sat at the table.

"I once saw a sign on a camper that said 'If this trailer's rockin', don't bother knockin'.''

"That's very crude," Jessi told him, venting some of her ire at being caught in this ridiculous, uncomfortable situation.

"Then I'm sorry I said it," Gabe replied. "I just thought it was funny." His expression told Jessi that she'd hurt his feelings. Though regretful, she hadn't the energy to apologize, and, to make matters worse, her headache had suddenly returned full force—surely a response to the tension knotting every muscle in her body.

Without a word, Jessi turned and retrieved the first aid kit from the cabinet for the second time that day.

"What are you doing?" Gabe asked.

"Getting some aspirin."

"You still have that headache?" He sounded worried.

"I got rid of it for a while, but now it's back." She took a bottle of aspirin out of the kit and opened it.

"Take one of these instead," Gabe said, his voice so close that Jessi jumped. She hadn't heard him join her. He dug into the box and pulled out a packet of tablets. "They work better...so much better, in fact, that half a tablet is probably all a woman of your body build would need."

Jessi felt *his* body build—oh, so male—close behind her and eased a little to the left so the two of them wouldn't actually touch.

"Thanks," she murmured, ignoring his advice and surreptitiously swallowing a whole tablet. If it made her sleep, then so much the better. "Now if you don't mind, I think I'll go to bed. I'm really exhausted."

"You mean you don't want to stay up with me for a while?" She heard his disappointment. "We could watch the late show or play cards or—"

"No." Jessi made herself look him in the eye. "Thanks for the four-leaf clover. Maybe my luck will change for the better, and maybe, even though you've given this to me,

yours won't change for the worse." That said, she walked
to the bedroom and shut the door.

Jessi heard Gabe mutter something that sounded suspiciously like "already has," but ignored him. It served the
man right to spend the night alone. He had lied to her, or
if not exactly that, had certainly omitted telling her something very important.

She still wondered why.

Stepping out of her jeans, pulling her shirt over her head,
Jessi made short work of stripping down for the night. In
the process, she broke her flower necklace, which she'd
forgotten: suddenly blue, she actually cried a little as she
set the necklace carefully aside and then slipped into her
oversized sleep shirt.

Seconds later she doused the lantern and crawled between the sheets in a room so dark she couldn't see her
own hand when she held it inches from her nose. Though
the occasional flashes of lightning relieved the deep black-
ness, Jessi came to dread them since deafening thunder always followed.

She thought of her daughter, but didn't worry. Anna Kate
loved storms. In fact, the harder the rain, the louder the
thunder, the better. Besides…it felt good to have the bed
to herself for a change, if oddly lonely. Luckily, the tablet
Jessi had swallowed kicked in before long and she actually
relaxed enough to doze.

But deep sleep eluded her…or were the scattered, scary
thoughts whirling inside her head really nightmares?

She found herself running through a forest. Rain poured
down so that her clothes and hair clung, and though her
temples pounded with pain, she could not stop because
someone—a man—chased her. Suddenly Jessi saw a cave.
She ran for the shelter and ducked into it only to spy a
glowing box. Pursuit now forgotten, she opened the box,
which held a jumble of things that all seemed to matter—
a photo, flowers, a four-leaf clover.

Thunder rolled. Distracted from her find, Jessi turned and

saw the silhouette of a man framed by the eerie glow of lightning at the mouth of the cave. She screamed, a sound drowned by another peal of thunder.

The man rushed forward and grabbed Jessi, who fought him for her life even though dizzy, disoriented and tethered to the cave floor.

"Jessi!" he exclaimed.

Though vaguely familiar, the voice offered no comfort and, in fact, frightened Jessi even more since this threatening stranger knew her name. Somehow Jessi freed her legs and feet of what bound them and then kicked him hard in the side.

"Go away!" she cried. "Get out!"

To her astonishment and relief, he immediately backed off. His features almost devilish in the iridescent flashes of lightning, he turned sharply to exit the room.

The room? *The room?*

Jessi's nightmare swiftly receded into the shadows. Her heart rate began to slow. Reality returned.

The room took on a familiar look, and memory clicked in. Jessi glanced around, recognizing her surroundings, and realized it had all been a bad dream...or had it? Suddenly unsure of just what had been dream and what truth, she scrambled out of the bed and threw open her door.

"Gabe?" she called, venturing into the kitchen, her only light the intermittent lightning.

An especially intense flash revealed his empty bed.

At once, Jessi knew the identity of her pursuer and guessed that he hadn't been pursuing at all, but simply trying to check on her. Mortified, she remembered how she'd kicked him. She tried to imagine where he could have gone on such a night. Only one possibility came to mind—his truck. Another flash of lightning and a peek out the rain-splashed window confirmed her guess.

Without hesitation or umbrella, Jessi dashed from the trailer and ran barefoot through the pouring rain to the truck. She pounded on Gabe's window, visibly startling him, though he quickly recovered and opened the truck door.

"What the hell are you doing?" he demanded even as he scooted across the seat and helped her climb into the truck beside him.

Out of breath, drenched, Jessi couldn't even reply for several seconds. "I'm…trying…to…apologize. I didn't… know what…I was doing. It was a…dream. No, a nightmare. I'm sorry."

"It's me who's sorry," muttered Gabe. "You've been afraid of me from the first. I knew it. I should never have burst into your bedroom like that."

"But I'm not afraid of y-y-ou," Jessi responded, her teeth chattering. She shivered violently from head to toe.

Gabe spat out a curse and slipped out of his long-sleeved flannel shirt, which left him wearing a T-shirt and a pair of sweatpants.

"Put this on," he ordered, thrusting the garment at her. Jessi obeyed, then immediately shivered again.

With another curse, Gabe reached out to pull her across the seat to him. Wrapping one arm around her back and slipping the other under her legs, he lifted her onto his lap and then held her close.

Jessi cherished the heavenly contact and clung to him, her face buried against his neck. Gabe was dry, warm, safe…everything she needed right then and maybe forever.

"I'd never hurt you. Never," he murmured, tightening the embrace, rocking their bodies in a strangely comforting way that was old as time itself.

"I know that. I always have."

Clearly doubting what she said, Gabe stopped all movement and tucked a finger under Jessi's chin to raise her face, almost as if he could peer through her eyes straight into her heart.

Jessi cooperated fully, making use of this opportunity to do a little soul-searching of her own. She read Gabe's concern; she read his confusion; she read his passion. He wanted to kiss her. She knew it at once even though he made no move to do so, perhaps out of fear that she would run.

But running was the last thing on Jessi's mind right now, and she wanted Gabe to know.

Without a word of warning, Jessi framed Gabe's face in her hands and pressed her lips to his. He responded at once, kissing not just her mouth, but her cheeks, her chin and her forehead. As he kissed her face, he touched her body— firm, possessive caresses that tantalized and made Jessi wild with wanting more.

More is what Gabe gave her. More kisses, placed where his hands had touched. More caresses to flesh that heated in response. No longer chilled, Jessi shrugged out of Gabe's flannel shirt, then peeled off her own sopping nightshirt. She next helped Gabe out of his.

The windows began to fog. Gabe moaned softly when Jessi's fingernails raked his pectorals. He palmed her bare breasts, paying particular attention to the tips, which hardened to his touch. Gabe then guided Jessi back on the seat, going with her until she lay cradled in his arms, her legs over his thighs, her feet against the door. Gabe, his own feet still on the floor, kissed Jessi then, and, with his free hand, resumed exploration of her breasts, her abdomen and the lace of her panties.

So good, so right, Jessi thought as Gabe moved his lips over her lips and slipped his hand under the elastic waistband of her bikinis.

So right?

Gabe's fingers dipped between her legs.

This?

Yes…oh yes. At least the moves. But the location…well, it was all wrong. She and Gabe should be in a bed somewhere instead of this cramped, damp pickup truck. They should be warm, dry, naked.

Naked?

Raising her hands to her temples, Jessi pressed hard to clear her fuzzy head.

"Are you okay?" Gabe asked.

"Yes…no…I'm not sure."

"You still have your headache, don't you?"

Jessi started to deny it, then realized Gabe had just provided the perfect escape route from this precarious situation.

Not that she wanted to escape. She didn't…now. But something told Jessi that the bright light of dawn might give her a different perspective.

"Yes, even though I took a whole tablet instead of a half."

"You took a whole one? Damn, Jessi, no wonder you had nightmares." Gabe slipped his hand out from under her head and sat back up.

He took Jessi with him, then didn't touch her again…at least not with his hands. His bare chest felt as wonderfully hard to her sensitized breasts as another part of his anatomy—a part she'd yet to explore—felt to her backside.

Jessi gulped and wrapped her arms around his neck. "What are you doing?"

Gabe didn't answer for what seemed an eternity, and when he finally did, his words came out a hoarse whisper. "You need to go back to bed."

"Alone?"

"Bingo."

"Are you sure?" She couldn't keep from running her hands over his muscled shoulders, tracing his Adam's apple with her finger.

"I'm sure."

Jessi sighed. "You're an honorable man, Gabe."

He laughed—a sound bereft of humor—and handed her his flannel shirt, now rumpled and damp. "Don't press your luck, babe."

Babe. That word again, and this time Jessi loved it.

"We never talked," she said as she obediently slipped

into his flannel shirt and buttoned it from neck to hem. Though Jessi had once dreaded the thought of intimate conversation with Gabe, at this moment she realized the necessity.

But Gabe just laughed again, this time honestly amused. "Not tonight."

"But—"

"Not tonight."

She frowned at his gruff tone and only belatedly acknowledged the sweat beading his brow, the tension in his body, the way he kept his hands flat to the truck seat. Clearly Gabe walked the fine line between passion and self-control. Jessi realized she'd do well not to jostle him.

"Later, then," she murmured, snatching up her abandoned nightshirt, sliding off his lap and then getting out of the truck.

Jessi dashed through the still-pouring rain to the trailer, Gabe one step behind. Her wet, bare feet slipped on the linoleum floor of the kitchen, and she would've fallen if Gabe hadn't caught her.

He clasped strong hands on Jessi's upper arms, setting her on her feet. She, in turn, clutched his biceps. Their gazes locked. Gabe groaned softly and kissed her—hard—on the lips even as he ran his hands over her breasts, his touch searing her flesh as though the thick flannel shirt weren't even there. Then Gabe raised the back of that rain-splattered shirt, and, grasping the elastic waistband of her panties, lowered them down over her hips so he could trace those curves of flesh and squeeze them.

His touch felt almost rough and oh so heavenly. Suddenly weak in the knees, Jessi pressed her mouth to his heart, which thudded as erratically as hers.

"Go to bed, Jessi." His words sounded very much like a warning.

"In a minute." His chest muffled her words.

"No, now." Gabe pulled her panties up with a stinging snap of elastic.

A flash of lightning revealed his tortured expression, how very close he'd come to losing control. Shocked by his intensity, yet certain she'd love anything he did to her, Jessi stepped obediently back and pivoted toward the bedroom.

But Gabe caught her arm, halting escape. In slow motion, he lowered his face to hers and kissed her again, his probing tongue a sensual hint of the mating they both desired. Jessi opened her mouth to him, savoring the flavor, encouraging him even as her fingers found and boldly traced that part of his anatomy she needed most.

He groaned and tipped his head back. "Leave, Jessi. Now. *Please.*"

Somehow Jessi found the strength that Gabe could not. Releasing him, slipping free of his embrace, she stepped back and then turned to run for the safety of the bedroom.

Friday morning came too soon. Jessi glanced at her face in the mirror upon rising and moaned. Mrs. Grim Reaper would look better today, thanks to Jessi's midnight meandering and her intimate, yet unconsummated, encounter with Gabe.

Hastily, she brushed her hair and put on makeup, something she hadn't really felt the need for out in the woods, but which today seemed critical. Jessi then agonized over what to wear, finally choosing a fitted white T-shirt and a pair of jeans that she especially liked.

Gabe will appreciate this, she decided, a thought that made her look in the mirror again. She saw a woman who might be in love; she saw a woman who wished last night had ended differently.

She also saw a woman whose thin T-shirt revealed what the memory of Gabe Dillard's touch could do to the tips of her breasts. With a curse of annoyance, Jessi snatched up a blue chambray shirt and slipped it on over the T-shirt as a jacket. As she walked out of the bedroom she rolled up the long sleeves.

In the kitchen, she found Gabe already awake and sitting

at the table, watching the morning news. He looked gorgeous in jeans and a pullover shirt that matched his eyes. She smiled at him. He smiled right back.

At once another area of Jessi's body, an area below the waist, began to tingle. Not a result of memories, this sensation, she realized, but a complaint of his neglect or maybe a plea for his attention.

Criminy, she thought, turning her back on Gabe so she could get control of her lusty thoughts and start cooking breakfast. She found a skillet of sizzling bacon already on the stove and biscuits in the oven.

"My way of apologizing about last night," Gabe said.

At once Jessi's spirits took a nosedive. He regretted what had happened between them?

"It's okay," she somehow managed to blurt. "I guess the storm made us both a little crazy."

"Yeah," he said, getting to his feet and joining her. "Normally I would've knocked on your bedroom door, but for some reason I just barged on in...."

Abruptly realizing to what Gabe's apology really referred, Jessi sagged against the counter with relief, a reaction not lost on her companion.

"You thought I was sorry about everything else, didn't you?"

"Yes."

"Well, I'm not," he told her, stepping close, brushing his lips over hers. "And I think it's high time for that talk."

Before Jessi could agree, the front door rattled and Anna Kate burst into the trailer.

"Good morning, sunshine," Jessi said, turning quickly away from Gabe. "How'd you sleep?"

"Real good," her daughter replied. "Did you and Gabe have fun?"

"We sure did," Jessi answered, as much for the benefit of August and Shari, now stepping into the trailer, as for Anna Kate. "Good morning, you two. I see you survived a night with Anna Kate."

"We had a great time," Shari responded.

August, however, said nothing, and one glance at him told Jessi he wasn't likely to. Clearly yesterday's disappointment had spilled over into today. In fact, he looked to be in a worse mood, if possible. She hoped this funk did not result from Anna Kate's sleepover, and vowed to ask Shari the first moment she could.

That came minutes after, when the men sat at the table and began to talk about the day's plans while the women finished cooking.

"Is everything okay?" Jessi asked.

Shari just shrugged.

"Anna Kate didn't—"

"A.K. was a doll."

Jessi sighed her relief. At least August's blue mood wasn't her daughter's fault.

Nonetheless, everyone paid for it at breakfast during which August found first one reason and then another to snap at each of them in turn. Toward the end of the meal, Jessi saw the muscle in Gabe's jaw begin to twitch—a sure sign he wanted to say something to his grumpy employer, but held back. She tried to lighten the mood, but was rewarded for her efforts with August's glare.

"Oh, don't be such a grouch!" Shari finally blurted, words that shocked everyone but August into silence.

"What am I supposed to do?" her husband growled back. As usual, he and Shari sat together on one side of the table while Gabe, Jessi and Anna Kate sat opposite them.

"You're supposed to *lead* us, to set an example by keeping your chin up even though we've had a little setback."

"Setback?" August roared. "You call finding two strongboxes full of junk a 'setback'?"

"That *junk* as you call it, probably meant the world to those two miners."

"Yeah, well, they were fools, just like you four are for

coming along on this misbegotten, badly-planned treasure hunt of mine.''

"What do you mean, 'badly-planned'?" Shari retorted. "You have the best guide money can buy, a wonderful cook, all the latest equipment—''

"And enough rain to float Noah's ark.''

"So what's a little rain?" Shari, not the least intimidated by her husband's temper, stuck her face right in his.

"Rain means delay, Shari. I can't afford a delay.''

"Why not?" she demanded. "We're not on a deadline.''

"Maybe you're not," he answered. "But I am...I am.''

Shari blinked at him. "You mean you've already found someone to publish this treasure book?''

"I'm talking about my life." His voice boomed in the close confines of the trailer. "My career. Our marriage. It's all going down the drain a mile a minute, and I can't do anything to stop it.''

Shari's eyes widened with disbelief even as Jessi and Gabe exchanged an uh-oh look. "What are you talking about? Nothing's going down the drain...not your life, not your career and certainly not our marriage.''

August laughed—a brittle sound that revealed his doubt and hinted at the imminence of an out-and-out free-for-all.

Noting that her daughter's eyes were already wider than Shari's, Jessi came to life, sliding out of the eating booth and taking Anna Kate's hand to urge her to do the same. Not surprisingly, Gabe followed, and the three of them quickly left the trailer to give Shari and August some privacy.

Just as Gabe shut the trailer door, Shari and August began to shout at each other in earnest. Anna Kate, clearly subdued, glanced from her mother to her stepdad as if for reassurance. Jessi gave it at once, scooping up her daughter and hugging her tight.

"Don't be upset," she whispered. "They aren't going to hurt each other. They just have to clear up some misunderstandings.''

"What's a misserstanding?" Anna Kate asked.

"Mis-under-standing." Jessi frowned, trying to come up with an answer a four-year-old would understand.

"It's when two people don't think alike," Gabe smoothly interjected. He stood just behind Anna Kate and Jessi. When the girl craned her neck to see around her mother's head, Gabe stepped closer so that he stood beside them. "People should try to get along all the time, of course, but often they just can't. When that happens, it's best to talk about the problem."

"But Shari and August are yelling."

Gabe grimaced. "So they are. Hmm..." His eyes begged Jessi for help on this one.

"Sometimes when people get excited they raise their voices. Remember when you and Heather got Barbie dolls alike, and you thought she had yours, but she didn't?"

Anna Kate nodded.

"Remember how you yelled at her?"

Anna Kate nodded again.

"That's kind of what August and Shari are doing. I suspect they'll both be sorry later and kiss and make up, just like you and Heather did."

"You and daddy never did."

Jessi frowned. "When did I ever raise my voice to Gabe?"

"Not *him* daddy," Anna Kate replied, rolling her expressive violet eyes. "My real one...that we divorced."

Jessi felt the color drain from her face. Anna Kate remembered those awful fights with Les? Why, she was just a baby at the time...barely over a year old. Disconcerted that she and her ex may have traumatized their precious daughter for life, Jessi raised her gaze to Gabe, whose expression revealed his sympathy.

He opened his mouth to speak, but before he could, the trailer door slammed back and Shari stomped out to head, for all appearances, for her own trailer. August burst out the door seconds later...just in time to hear his truck start up. He froze mid-step, a look of shock on his face, then bounded toward where he'd parked it the day before, just out of sight behind the Dillard trailer.

But before he could get there, Shari drove the vehicle past them all and then right out of camp, tires spinning on the wet, leaf-strewn ground and throwing up clumps of mud.

"Well, hell!" August exploded, staring after her.

Anna Kate slapped her hand to her mouth and turned wide eyes to her mother, who almost laughed aloud at August's utter disbelief. Definitely more sympathetic with Shari, Jessi felt little sympathy for her gruff employer, who now looked quite pitiful and for once unsure of what to do.

Gabe didn't share August's problem. "Catch!" he exclaimed, tossing his truck keys to August.

That giant of a man's face lit right up when he caught them, and a heartbeat later he was behind the wheel of Gabe's truck, starting up the powerful engine. It roared to life at once and August shifted gears and guided the vehicle down the trail. Almost instantly man and truck vanished into the thick woods...leaving Gabe, Jessi and Anna Kate staring after them in silent wonder.

"I hope he remembers to buckle up," Anna Kate murmured, words that made both Gabe and Jessi burst into laughter.

When they finally stopped, Jessi became aware of the intense, unnatural silence of camp. For long moments not a sound could be heard, then the chirp of a bird signaled a return to normalcy that culminated in the steady *plop! plop!* of raindrops on leaves.

"Uh-oh." Gabe glanced up through the tree tops at a decidedly stormy sky, then reached for Anna Kate, who slipped her arm around his neck. Unfortunately, the girl didn't release her mother. As a result, Jessi took a stumbling step and found her face inches from Gabe's.

"Are they coming back?" Anna Kate asked without loosening her hold on them.

"They'd better," Gabe answered, his gaze locked with Jessi's. "He's got my truck."

Chapter Ten

For hours slipped by while Gabe and Jessi puttered around the trailer and Anna Kate watched Shari's television, then played house with her bear and doll in the bedroom. It rained hard for about half that time, but finally slowed to a sprinkle that kept the air cool, yet not so cool that Gabe couldn't open all the camper windows.

He relished the sounds of the forest and thought about Washington and the land he would soon own on the Snake River. He also thought about his future, in particular the plans he'd made, all of them custom-designed for a father and son.

Would his plans stretch to accommodate a mother and her daughter, too? he wondered, his speculative gaze on Jessi. She stood at the open door just then, her back to him, leaning on the jamb and gazing outside.

A feeling of affection came over Gabe, so powerful that it took his breath and made him wonder if he might be in love. Having never really been there before, he couldn't say for sure. He did know he couldn't bear the thought of losing Jessi, which was exactly what would happen if he didn't take steps to keep their lives linked.

He tried to imagine a day without her, and couldn't. She was that much a part of him now. He next tried to remember exactly what her plans for the future were, but couldn't do that, either.

Because her plans weren't as definite as his?

Maybe, Gabe decided, recalling only that Jessi intended to get out of debt and open a cafe or some such. He didn't think she'd actually picked the location for this eatery yet. He didn't even think she knew just what kind of place it would be. He did know she wanted to work for herself, a goal he could certainly understand, and that she did not need a man in her life.

Damn the luck.

"Ever thought about living in Washington?" Gabe's question just asked itself, leaving him as startled as Jessi appeared to be when she glanced over her shoulder at him.

"No, though I'll bet it's pretty."

"Actually it's more *beautiful* than pretty."

"Hmm." She smiled and left the door to slip into the booth opposite him. "And Snake River is the garden spot?"

"Exactly."

"Then lucky you."

"Yeah…lucky me."

"You sound a little down. Is something wrong?" She seemed honestly concerned.

"Nah. I was just thinking about when this treasure hunt is over, and I realized I'm going to miss you and Anna Kate."

"No kidding?" She looked pleased.

"No kidding. Will you miss me?"

"Well, I have gotten used to having you underfoot," Jessi teased.

"Thanks a million."

Jessi laughed. "I'm certain Anna Kate will miss her

Daddy G. And, to be honest, I think I'll miss you, too. You've been a good friend.''

"I could've been more to you. Still can." Again his own words surprised him.

"What do you mean *still can?* You know how difficult it is to get a moment alone." She glanced toward the bedroom where Anna Kate could be heard singing sleepily to her toys.

Gabe's jaw dropped. Was Jessi saying that she'd thought about a sexual relationship with him? That she might even go for it?

"Actually," he answered, keeping his voice level and his tone matter-of-fact, "I was referring to later...after we get our money and return to civilization."

"You're not going back to Washington?"

"Oh, I'm going back."

"Then when...?" Her voice trailed to silence. Her eyes narrowed in speculation. "You want me to go with you to the Snake River."

It was a statement, not a question.

"I'd like that, yes." There, he'd said it.

"As what...your lover?"

Gabe shrugged. "My lover...or we could stay husband and wife if that would make you feel more comfortable."

"You mean make our marriage *legal?*" She sounded shocked.

"Surely the thought has crossed your mind." He deliberately challenged her, going on gut instinct that told him women, natural nest-builders that they were, couldn't help but think about possibilities. Why, he'd even done that, himself.

"Maybe," Jessi murmured, confessing nothing.

"Admit it, Jessi," Gabe said. "You've thought about what it would be like to be married to me, probably more than once."

"And if I have?"

"What did you decide?"

"I realized if my first marriage had been half as much fun as this pretend one, I'd probably still be with Les." Jessi reached out and touched Gabe's hand, which rested on the table. "You're a good man, Gabe. You dream big and work hard. You appreciate the worth of family. I think you'd make a great husband."

"Your husband?" Gabe couldn't resist asking.

"I honestly don't know. I do know that I'm afraid if we made the marriage legal and then things didn't work out, I'd never get over it. Neither would Anna Kate. You heard her earlier when she said she remembered Les and me fighting. The last thing she needs are more emotional scars."

"You're assuming the worst."

"How can I help it? You and I are in lust, not love. How can a marriage survive if the man and woman aren't in love?"

Glad he hadn't shared his deepening feelings, Gabe murmured, "Love is highly overrated and, besides, it didn't save your first marriage."

"Maybe that's because what I felt for Les wasn't true love."

Gabe snorted at that. "What the hell *is* true love, Jessi? Tell me that."

"It's love that's meant to be. It's destiny." The moment Jessi uttered that last dramatic word, she tensed visibly. Clearly rattled—and Gabe couldn't imagine why—she got up from the table and walked once again to the door, where she stood for long moments, her back to him, but obviously disconcerted.

Curious, Gabe joined her there and stood beside her. "What is it? What's wrong?"

"I just remembered something Shari said to me…something about destiny."

"Which was…?"

"If you can't explain why you're attracted to someone, then that someone is probably your destiny."

"That's hogwash."

She looked relieved to hear him say that. "I think so, too."

"Was this conversation with Shari the reason for our destiny discussion in the truck that day we drove to Neely Bend?"

Jessi nodded and gave him a sheepish smile.

"And what was the reason for the conversation with Shari?"

"She said that *you* were *my* destiny."

"Bull."

"Of course."

"I know exactly why I'm attracted to you."

"You do?"

"Sure…because you're so beautiful."

"And my, um, beauty is the reason you think we should make our marriage legal?" She looked uncomfortable with the offhanded compliment and maybe a bit doubtful, too. "Does this mean when I'm old and gray you'll kick me out?"

"Looks don't mean a thing to me!" Gabe retorted, then winced. "So maybe your looks aren't what attract me. Maybe it's your mind."

"I could lose that, too. Will you kick me out then?"

"I'd never kick you out," Gabe said.

"Then my mind isn't really so important, is it?"

"No."

"So what really attracts you to me, Gabe?"

"Damned if I know," he admitted.

Long silence followed that confession. Then Jessi turned slightly and placed her hands on Gabe's chest. Her gaze found his.

"You asked me if I'd thought about staying married to you. Well, I have, and I honestly don't know if it would work. I have another idea, though, and I'd like to bounce it off you…if you don't mind?"

"I don't mind," Gabe muttered, intrigued by her serious tone.

"How would you feel about my investing in your Snake River enterprise and running your café?"

Gabe couldn't believe his ears. "You mean be my business partner?"

Jessi nodded. "My money would get you what you want faster. I think we'd work well together, and it would give us more time to get acquainted with one another."

"I don't know...," Gabe murmured, not lying. Her proposal had caught him off guard. "I had you figured for the independent type. You've surprised me."

"Even independent types have to work. I think you need my money and my skill."

"You're damned right I do." Gabe caught Jessi by the waist. "So you want to invest in my business."

She smiled. "Yes."

"Will you also invest in my life?"

"Meaning...?"

"Be my friend?"

"I'm that already."

"What about being my family? I need that as much as your money, your skill and your friendship."

She laughed softly and shook her head, obviously still confused. *"Meaning...?"*

"Make the marriage legal?"

She hesitated so long he thought she never would answer. "Maybe."

This time it was Gabe who laughed and shook his head. "Meaning...?"

"Can I be your partner without making the marriage legal?"

So she still didn't want to be his wife. Gabe marveled at the intensity of his disappointment, disappointment that did much to convince him he'd fallen for her.

Damn.

"I'm not sure I'd be able to keep my hands off you. It could be awkward."

"Promises, promises," she teased, her smile sassy.

"No, seriously. Looking and not touching gets old fast."

"You're telling me?"

Gabe ignored that. "And I don't want to do it anymore."

Jessi thought for a moment. "So you think marriage will agree with you?"

"It will," Gabe said. "It has."

"And is that the reason you didn't tell August the truth when he apologized for making us get married?"

So she knew about that. Why wasn't he surprised? "Shari told you."

"Yes."

"When?"

"On my birthday, and it was a nasty shock."

Gabe swallowed hard. "I know I should've 'fessed up, but I was afraid...I mean I thought..." Gabe sighed. "I liked being married, okay? It felt good having family, even if they were a lie."

"Anna Kate and I might make a family man out of you yet," Jessi murmured, leaning closer.

"Please try," Gabe answered and then covered her mouth with his. Their kiss was long and sweet. A promise of more things to come?

And when? he next wondered, envisioning the two of them at his home in Washington. They'd put their children to bed, then slip outside with a blanket and make love under the stars.

Love? Oh yeah.

Did he dare tell Jessi? Gabe wondered.

"Actually not being in love could prove an advantage to our relationship," Jessi murmured just then, brushing her mouth along his jawline. Her words felt warm on his skin, yet cold to his heart.

"Why?" asked Gabe, oh so glad he hadn't tried to verbalize the emotions he felt right then.

"Because we're less likely to break each other's hearts if we're not in love. Oh, it's probably too late for Anna Kate, who already adores you, but you and I can take out a mutual need, no-love insurance policy on each other, absolutely guaranteeing that our relationship, whatever we choose it to be, will work."

"You think?"

"I know. Look, Gabe, I need your café, your moral support and your companionship. Anna Kate needs a dad. You need my money, my talent, my daughter and—"

"Your sex." Gabe glanced toward the bedroom to locate Anna Kate, who'd stopped singing. He spied her lying on the bed with her stuffed pals, for all appearances snoozing. Turning his and Jessi's bodies so that his body blocked Anna Kate's view—just in case the child woke—Gabe slipped his hand under Jessi's T-shirt and palmed one lace-encased breast, then the other. Jessi rewarded his efforts with her sexy sigh.

"Touching *is* more fun than just looking, isn't it?" she whispered, tracing his bulging fly with her fingers.

Gabe shivered and swallowed hard, a reaction that made Jessi tip her head back and smile. Then that sexy smile faded and her brows knitted in a slight frown. "What was that?"

"What was what?" Gabe asked, dipping his head to nuzzle the flesh just below her earlobe.

"I hear something."

Her words barely penetrated his sexual fog. His hands continued their lazy exploration of her body. "What?"

"*I hear something.* Be quiet." She put a finger to his lips.

Gabe kissed it.

"Did you hear that? Did you?" She pounded on his shoulder with her fist to snap him out of his daze, then captured his roaming hands in hers.

Sighing impatiently, Gabe shifted his attention from Jessi's delectable neck to her face. "Okay. All right. I'm listening."

Bzzzzz.

Gabe frowned. What the hell...?

Bzzzzz.

"The cell phone!" he exclaimed, abruptly releasing Jessi and dashing out the door to the Taylor camper. In seconds he snatched up the phone, which he'd never have heard if the Taylors' windows hadn't been open, the door ajar, and the rain just a sprinkle. "Hello?"

"Gabe, it's August."

"What's up?" Gabe asked, at once all seriousness.

"Shari and I are at a motel a few miles south. I...we... well, I think we'll be here all night. We need to get some things sorted out."

The understatement of the year.

"Will you three be okay without your truck?"

"We've got first aid, we've got food, we've got a phone. Yeah, we'll be all right."

"Good...good." August sounded a bit distracted. "Look, man, I'm sorry about this."

"No sweat."

"I'll give you and Jessi a bonus—"

"You're paying us too much already."

"We'll discuss this tomorrow, okay?"

"Sure," Gabe told him.

Without a goodbye, August hung up the phone, leaving Gabe to marvel at how much more human his employer had sounded in just that two-minute conversation. What had Shari done to him? Gabe had to wonder, knowing that whatever it was had worked a miracle.

Tucking the phone in his pocket, Gabe glanced around the trailer to see if everything was okay. He noted that rain had come in the open windows at some time during the day, so he found a towel to clean up the water. Then, after closing everything up tight, he walked back to his camper.

It took only seconds to catch Jessi up on the latest. She seemed disconcerted by the news...or did the knowledge that they'd be alone until tomorrow upset her?

"This would be a good time to practice being married,"

Gabe said as he slipped onto the bench seat in the eating booth and turned on the television to catch the noon news.

"Excuse me?"

"We'll pretend we've made this marriage legal and are living together in Washington." He gave her a grin. "You do remember how to pretend?"

"I've been doing it all week, haven't I?"

Gabe nodded. "And doing it well. So today I'm your real husband and you're my real wife. And tonight—"

"Our real daughter will be sleeping with me, as usual."

"But she'd rather sleep on this bed." He patted the kitchen table.

"Almost certainly," Jessi smoothly agreed. "But she's still sleeping with me."

He sighed. "Whatever you say, ma'am."

Jessi laughed at that atypical reply. "So the pretending has already begun?"

Gabe looked at his watch. "As...of...*now!*"

Still laughing at his foolishness, Jessi opened up the cabinet and began to peruse the food stock, trying to decide what to prepare for lunch.

Gabe turned his attention to the television...or tried to. He found his thoughts kept jumping back to the Snake River, and he began to wonder if his ESP had kicked in, telling him he should call home.

Finally, after ten minutes of wondering that fast became worrying, Gabe took the cellular phone out of his shirt pocket, turned it on, and punched out the phone number of his friend back in Washington.

That old friend answered on the second ring. "Hello?"

"Yo, Jerry. Gabe here. How's it going?"

"Fine...fine," Jerry Clark answered. "Are you rich yet?"

Gabe laughed and then showed the phone to Jessi, who'd turned around to find out—judging by her startled expression—who on earth he was talking to. "Nah, and won't be for a couple more weeks."

"I can wait."

"You'd better. Uh, is everything all right there?"

"Sure, why do you ask?"

"Just a feeling."

"Not another one of those!" Jerry exclaimed, laughing.

Gabe bore the good-natured teasing in silence, knowing, as Jerry did, that his sixth sense sometimes proved beneficial. "Yeah…another one of those."

"Everything is all right here. You did get a phone call from some lawyer, but—"

"A lawyer! *I got a call from a lawyer?*"

Jessi turned around again, no doubt in response to the panic in Gabe's voice. But Gabe couldn't help his overreaction. His worst nightmare involved Ryder's current foster parents, who were wonderful, loving people, deciding to adopt the child. Though that generous couple knew of Gabe's intentions to adopt Ryder himself and even seemed to support the plan, Gabe had always harbored a secret fear they might change their minds.

"That's right. Some guy named Edward Logan Stiles. I've got his number. You're supposed to call him when you get back in town."

"Did he mention Ryder?"

"No." Jerry hesitated, obviously picking up on Gabe's discomfiture. "Maybe I should give you the number now."

"Yeah. Do that." Gabe turned to Jessi, who now stood at his elbow, obviously concerned. "Got a piece of paper and a pencil?"

Jessi reached for her purse and, from it, retrieved a small spiral notebook and a pen.

"I'm ready," Gabe said to Jerry, who gave him the number. Gabe read it back. "I'll call him today."

"Okay…and would you call *me* back if something is wrong?"

"Yeah, sure," Gabe promised. Seconds later he was off the cell phone and staring at the numbers, almost afraid to dial them.

"What's up?" Jessi asked, slipping into the booth opposite him.

Before Gabe could answer, Anna Kate walked back into the room, rubbing her sleepy eyes. The girl crawled right up into Jessi's lap and buried her face in her mother's breast, an action that made Gabe's stomach knot with anxiety.

Was he never going to have a child of his own?

Quietly, he told Jessi about the lawyer's call.

"Don't wonder," she softly advised. "Call him."

"I think I'll call Ryder first," Gabe answered, already punching out the familiar number.

Ryder's foster mother, Mary Beth Longing, answered the phone.

Gabe got right to the point. "Jerry Clark told me I got a call from a lawyer. Has something happened with Ryder?"

"Why, no. He's fine."

"And you still support my adopting him."

"Of course," Mary Beth told him, adding, "That's all Ryder talks about. Would you like to speak to him?"

"Yeah," Gabe answered, shoulders sagging with relief. "Yeah, I would."

Seconds later, the boy answered the phone. "Hi, Uncle Gabe."

"Hi, yourself," Gabe replied, expelling his pent-up breath in a long sigh. He felt Jessi's gaze and raised his to meet it. She smiled encouragement. "Did you get your surprise?"

"You sent me a surprise?"

"Yeah," Gabe told him. "You should get it today, or, at the latest, tomorrow. I think you'll like it." They talked about general things—Gabe's treasure hunt, Ryder's football games—then Gabe said, "I've got to go. I'm on someone else's phone."

"Are you coming to see me soon?" Ryder asked.

"Thanksgiving for sure," Gabe told him. "Maybe even sooner."

"Okay."

"I love you, Ryder."

"Love you, too...*dad*."

As Gabe punched the button that would end the call, he had to blink back tears. A child as precious as his Ryder deserved so much better a hand than life had dealt him. Gabe couldn't wait to make things right. And lost in his plans to do just that, he tucked the phone back in his pocket.

"Aren't you going to call this Stiles guy?" Jessi instantly asked.

"Oh yeah," Gabe answered, retrieving the phone. In truth, he didn't care if he called the man or not now that he knew Ryder wasn't involved in any way. But with a glance at the notepad Jessi had loaned him, Gabe punched out a new number. A man answered moments later.

"Ed Stiles."

"Mr. Stiles, this is Gabe Dillard. I understand you called."

"Why, yes, Mr. Dillard, I did. I have some good news for you, some very good news...." Thus began a conversation so incredible that Gabe soon did nothing but listen and could barely turn off the cell phone when the lawyer finally rang off, some fifteen minutes later.

Numb with shock, he raised his gaze to Jessi. "Did you get any of that?"

"You have a brother," she answered, her eyes bright with curiosity and excitement.

"A half brother," Gabe corrected, propping his elbows on the table and resting his head in his hands. "And a sister...a *twin* sister."

Jessi's smile lit her whole face and warmed him, too. "Oh, Gabe. Tell me everything."

With a glance at Anna Kate, who seemed to be sleeping again, Gabe got up from the table and began to pace the room. "I've told you about how my father abandoned my mother when he learned she was pregnant, haven't I?"

Jessi nodded.

"And how my mother then gave me up when I was born?"

Another nod.

"What I didn't know is that she had twins, a boy and a girl, and, according to Mr. Stiles, kept the girl, my sister—" he tried the word on again for size "—my sister...and named her Mariah."

"Is she alive?"

"Yes, but this lawyer hasn't located her yet."

"And your mother?"

"Died years ago, apparently."

"What about this half brother? Tell me about him."

"Apparently my father married right after he left my mother. He and his wife had a son shortly after and named him Reo...Reo Sampson. Reo didn't know about me until dear ol' dad's death a few months ago. Then he found some papers, contacted a lawyer, and began the search for his half siblings."

"What an honorable thing to do," Jessi murmured. She looked as shell-shocked as he felt and, now that he thought about it, not particularly thrilled. She slid out of the booth, laid her slumbering daughter on the love seat, and walked over to give him a hug. Her smile, though wide, did not reach her eyes. "This is wonderful. Just wonderful."

"Wonderful," he echoed, in somewhat of a daze. "And almost too much to comprehend." Feeling suddenly weak in the knees, he released Jessi and walked back to sit on one of the bench seats. He did not face the table or put his legs under it, so when Jessi joined him there, it was easy for him to coax her to sit on his lap instead of the bench opposite him. "I've gone from orphan to family man in a matter of seconds. Damn, Jessi." He shook his head, which swam dizzily with possibilities. "Damn."

She said nothing, but hugged him as if there were no tomorrow.

"There's more to the story, of course," he said. "I just don't know it."

Jessi still said nothing.

"I have about a million questions." He laughed, suddenly exhilarated. "But they can wait until I meet with this Stiles guy and my brother, I guess."

Still nothing.

"You know," Gabe said, so caught up in his musings that he barely registered Jessi's uncharacteristic, inappropriate quiet, "I've often thought there was another part of me somewhere. Oh, I know that sounds ridiculous, but there were times when I did...." He examined Jessi's expression. "You think I've lost it, don't you?"

She shook her head and tugged his laced fingers apart so she could slip free of his embrace and stand up. "I don't think you've lost it. Twins often have psychic connections. It's a proven fact."

Gabe laughed at that. "Yeah, well, I won't go *that* far, but I sure will be glad to meet her."

"And when, exactly, is this going to happen?"

A sharpness in her tone made him glance quickly up at her. Gabe took full note of her expression—cool—and her demeanor—solemn.

"I don't really know. Edward Stiles said he'd get back to me tomorrow. I gave him this cell phone number." Gabe saw that the light in Jessi's eyes had dimmed. "Is something wrong?"

"Nothing's wrong," she quickly responded...too quickly, in his opinion.

"You're sure?"

"Positive." She smiled at him again, this time with more sincerity. "I'm very happy for you. *Ver*—"

Anna Kate's scream shocked them both into silence. In a flash, Jessi and Gabe stood by the bed.

"Anna Kate!" Jessi exclaimed, bending over to shake

the girl, who apparently still slept, caught up in a nightmare. "Wake up!"

Whimpering, the child opened tear-filled eyes and gazed up at them.

"You were dreaming," Jessi said, sitting on the love seat and taking her daughter in her arms. "Tell me about it."

Anna Kate, a huge tear rolling down her cheek, just shook her head and hugged her mother hard. Gabe sat next to them so he could engulf both mother and child in a hug.

"Was a tiger after you?" he asked.

Anna Kate, clearly in no mood for any teasing, just shook her head again and buried her face in her mother's breast.

"A camel?"

Another shake of the head.

"A bear?"

Anna Kate raised her head and shook it yet again. Gabe noticed a hint of a smile.

"Hmm. A rhinoceros?"

Anna Kate huffed her opinion of his guesses. He noted a twinkle had replaced the tear in her eye. "There aren't any rhinosrusses around here."

"Then what on earth was it?" Gabe demanded.

"A spider," Anna Kate said and shuddered.

"A little bitty spider?" he asked.

"No, a big, black, fuzzy one." Anna Kate released her mother long enough to show him the size of the arachnid in question—baseball, at least.

Gabe didn't have to fake his own violent shiver. "Whew! No wonder you were scared. I would be, too."

By now giggling at his antics, Anna Kate twisted to face him and threw her arms around his neck. Joining in her mirth, which sounded much better than cries of fear, Gabe fell back on the love seat, taking mother and daughter with him.

They lay that way for several minutes, a decidedly cozy trio. Gabe cherished the closeness and thanked his lucky stars for this woman and child who'd entered his life for such an odd reason.

Destiny?

Oh yeah. Nothing else could produce such feelings of total rightness, joy and, yes, love. He needed nothing more to be happy forever, not his half brother or even a mystery twin. So what, he wondered, did Jessi need?

More important, could he give it to her?

"Are you okay now?" the woman in question asked her daughter, who lay sprawled over her stepfather and her mother with her cheek resting on Gabe's chest. Jessi, herself, lay half on Gabe, too, with her head on his shoulder and her breasts crushed against his side, a sensation he especially enjoyed.

Anna Kate nodded.

"And you aren't scared anymore?" Gabe asked.

Anna Kate shook her head.

"You know we're a family now," Gabe then said, as much to reassure her as to test her mother. "Families stick together even when there's a big fat spider around."

"You're silly," his stepdaughter responded, playfully pinching his nose. Her mother, to Gabe's consternation, said nothing.

"An' yur byudeeful," he answered, his pronunciation so distorted by the nose pinch that Anna Kate—and her mother, too—giggled some more.

Chapter Eleven

Since Jessi noticed Gabe watching her closely for the rest of the afternoon, she deliberately kept her smile handy and her spirits up. How could she do otherwise when he was so obviously thrilled—as anyone would be—about having a half brother and a twin sister?

The fact that their existence meant Gabe no longer needed Jessi and Anna Kate simply did not matter. And Jessi's subsequent worrying about her place in his life amounted to nothing more than selfishness, for which she berated herself constantly.

It also meant she'd fallen for him—no big surprise. From the beginning, she'd recognized the danger of their cohabitation. The question now was how far had she fallen? Halfway down? Or all the way?

Around three o'clock the rain completely stopped, so the three of them ventured outside, much to Jessi's relief, and hiked to a nearby creek Gabe and August had found the day before. Surging against its banks, it rolled and roiled today, thanks to the hours of downpour. Both Jessi and Gabe kept a close watch on Anna Kate.

Gabe explained about the rising flow and showed Anna Kate telltale watermarks on the trees along the bank. They guessed how high the water might get during the day, marking the spot on a tree with his pocket knife.

On the walk back, Gabe glanced down and found an arrowhead in the mud at his feet, a discovery that seemed to thrill him as much as it did Jessi and her daughter. All three began a careful search for others along the path and got so involved in their mini treasure hunt that a sudden heavy rainstorm caught them unawares.

Gabe led the mad dash back to camp. Laughing, all three of them burst into the camper, where they stood dripping puddles of rainwater on the kitchen floor. Gabe's gaze swept over Jessi's face and soaked hair, then dropped to her T-shirt, which clung to her flesh. There his gaze lingered so long that she began to suspect Gabe could see what she could feel—the tips of her breasts growing taut.

Hoping he'd chalk up the reaction to the chill and not his heated gaze, Jessi brushed past Gabe's soaked, gorgeous body, and found towels. Then she shut the bedroom door so she and Anna Kate could change into dry clothes.

While she helped her daughter dress, Jessi wished for time with Gabe—for time, the dark, a bed, and for privacy, precious privacy. Surely, she thought, if she and Gabe made love to each other all night he'd realize how happy she could make him, how much he needed her.

But no. A night of passion would not equate to making "love" at all...at least for *him*. Their mating would be a simple act of sex that might make him happy for the moment, but had little to do with long-term need.

As for her own feelings about such a sensual liaison...well, Jessi knew it would be more than simple sex to her. It would honestly be making love.

And to think she'd told Gabe she didn't love him.

What a joke...but he'd seemed to believe the line, even was glad of it, all the more reason to keep this secret she'd only just worked through, herself.

Love. Such a simple word. Such a complex problem.

Did Gabe love her back…even a little? Jessi just didn't know. Oh, he'd seemed to at times, sure, but he was like that—naturally affectionate and considerate. Good manners did not mean love. Neither did desire or even need.

Thank goodness he still needed her money. With all this newfound kin, he certainly didn't need her to be his family anymore.

Impatiently, Anna Kate snatched the long-sleeved pull-over top that Jessi held. That action brought Jessi back to the present, and, with a soft, ''Sorry,'' she helped her daughter slip on the cotton top. She then let Anna Kate out of the bedroom and began to change her own clothes.

Minutes later, Jessi, now dry and warm, stepped back into the kitchen area. She got right to work grilling cheese sandwiches, which she served a short time later with cream of tomato soup—a professed favorite meal of Gabe's. They finished their dinner around eight o'clock, then watched television for an hour, at which time Anna Kate announced that she wanted to go to bed.

''You're sleepy already?'' Jessi asked, surprised. Normally after napping during the day, Anna Kate was good until way past her usual bedtime.

But tonight the child nodded.

''Well, okay.'' Jessi got up from the table. ''I'll turn back the covers of our bed. You get your nightie.''

''I'm sleeping here,'' Anna Kate replied, patting the kitchen table.

Jessi turned back to her daughter, who wore her most stubborn look. ''And just where will Gabe sleep?''

''With you.''

''I see. Well, we've been through this before, and, for your information, Miss Priss, Gabe is not going to sleep with me. He is going to sleep in his very own bed. Now hop down, quick as a bunny.''

Anna Kate just shook her head.

With a smile of apology at Gabe, who watched with avid

interest, Jessi walked back to the table and grasped her daughter's hand. "Come on, now. No foolishness."

"I'm sleeping here. It's my turn." The four-year-old's eyes glinted with stubbornness.

"No, you aren't."

"I am."

"You aren't and that's that." Jessi used her sternest tone—the one that always worked.

"But—" began Anna Kate.

"I have an idea!" Gabe stepped between them. "Anna Kate will sleep here—" he slapped his hand on the table "—Jessi will sleep in there—" he pointed to the bedroom, then held up a hand to ward off her immediate protest "—and I will sleep in the Taylor camper."

Jessi, all ready to nix the plan, instead breathed a sigh of relief. "That's a good idea, but I want Anna Kate to understand she can't get her way just because she throws a tantrum."

"I think she knows that." Gabe turned to Anna Kate, his face serious. "Don't you?"

"Bingo!" Anna Kate exclaimed, nodding so hard her hair bounced.

It was all Jessi could do not to laugh.

"Now let me get your bed made." Gabe began to disassemble the table, only to have Anna Kate wave him away.

"I can do it."

With a nod of acquiescence, Gabe let her.

And ten minutes later found Anna Kate in her nightie, under the covers and happy as a bug in a rug. With a pitiful sigh, Gabe glanced toward the door. Clearly, he hoped Jessi would invite him to just stay there and share her bed. Squaring her shoulders, hiding her own regret, Jessi just pointed to the door.

With another pitiful sigh, this one even more exaggerated, Gabe left.

Jessi sat by her daughter, who'd snuggled into the blan-

kets with her bear. They talked for five minutes or so—
mainly so Jessi could be sure no more nightmares lurked—
before Jessi told her daughter three of their happiest bedtime stories.

Only when Anna Kate slumbered peacefully did Jessi
turn down all the lanterns but one, which she carried with
her into her bedroom. There, in the spooky shadows tossed
by the flickering light, she slipped out of her clothes and
into her own sleep shirt. She then sat on the edge of the
bed and stared at nothing for several long minutes.

The rattle of the front doorknob jerked her to attention.

Jessi sat in silence for a handful of seconds, heart pounding, waiting for a repeat of the sound.

Instead of a rattle, she heard a soft thump, thump…on
the bedroom window located at the head of the bed. Heart
now in her throat, Jessi crawled over the bed to reach it
and, after counting "One-two-three…now!" yanked back
the curtain to peer out.

A pair of eyes peered back at her. Jessi gasped, dropped
the curtain and fell back on the bed.

Thump! Thump! "Jessi. It's me! It's just me!"

Gabe.

Breaths ragged, feeling utterly foolish, Jessi scrambled
up to her knees on the bed and drew back the curtain again.

"What are you doing?" she demanded through the glass
of the small window.

"The other camper is locked. I need you to let me in
this one."

"You're just now figuring that out?"

"Let me in quick, Jessi! It's pouring."

And so it was, she realized somewhat belatedly, just then
hearing the rapid drumming on the tin roof. With a soft,
"Damn!" Jessi slipped off the bed and ran lightly to the
front door of the trailer, which she threw open. Gabe burst
into the kitchen a heartbeat later, bringing with him a blast
of chilly night air and the wet of rain.

"W-w-would you get me a towel?" he asked through chattering teeth. His whole body shivered.

Jessi complied, all the while wondering what explanation he could possibly have for the long delay between his leaving and his return—a good half hour. Silently, she handed him the requested towel.

Gabe dried his hair, which hung in spikes over his forehead, ears and neck, then mopped up his arms and face before taking his feet out of the leather deck shoes he wore around camp.

"I've got to get on some dry things," he murmured softly, quietly retrieving his usual sweats and T-shirt from where he stored them under the love seat. He then headed for the bedroom, followed by Jessi, who'd just that moment realized he'd never taken his sleep clothes with him the first time he left the trailer. She stepped right into the bedroom and shut the door softly behind her.

"Did you do all this on purpose?" she asked, now very suspicious about his whole sleep-in-the-Taylor-trailer idea.

"What?" Gabe pulled his soaked T-shirt over his head and dropped it on the linoleum. He next got rid of his socks.

"Did you know that trailer was locked?"

"Of course not."

"Then why didn't you take these with you when you left a while ago?" She pointed to the folded sweats, now lying on the bed.

"I didn't think about it."

"What have you been doing for the last thirty minutes?"

Gabe glared at her. "What is this? Twenty questions?" Deliberately, he unzipped his jeans. Jessi did not shift her gaze, but stared right back...even when he stepped out of the soaked denim and added that garment to the growing pile of wet things.

"I'm taking these off, too," Gabe warned, snapping the elastic waistband of the colorful boxer shorts he wore.

Silk? This rugged wilderness guide wore silk boxers? Fascinated by the unlikely event, Jessi didn't move until

Gabe actually began to lower the boxers, then whirled around so that she had her back to him. She heard the swish of silk, then a soft plop as the soaked undershorts hit the floor.

"You can turn around now," Gabe told her several seconds later.

Jessi waited several more before she peered over one shoulder, then turned her whole body to face him again. "I'm waiting."

"For what?" Gabe, dressed now in the familiar gray sweats, pulled on the ragged half T-shirt he always slept in.

"For an explanation. I want to know why you waited until Anna Kate was asleep before you came back."

"I did no such thing."

"Then where have you been for the last thirty minutes?"

"I walked to the creek again, okay?"

"In the dark? Why?"

"I wasn't sleepy. Damn, Jessi. What's the problem?"

Suddenly she felt silly for her suspicions. "Nothing. I just thought—"

"That I planned this whole bed thing so I could make a move on you? I thought we were past the point of tricks. I thought we were friends."

"We were—are."

"I also thought our desire was mutual."

"It is."

"But you don't trust me."

He looked hurt, and, she realized with regret, he had every right to be offended. Jessi sighed and turned her back on him to head to the door. Destination? She didn't know.

"It's me I don't trust, Gabe. Not you," she murmured, her hand on the knob, her back to the man. "And that is very upsetting. I thought I was in control. I thought I had a handle on my life, my emotions, my desires—" my heart "—but where you're concerned…" Slowly, she turned to face him again. "I think I'd better tell you something."

She walked back and sat on the bed, then patted it in invitation to Gabe.

He sat beside her.

"I hate to admit this—it's so, so selfish that I can't believe it—but I'm almost sorry your brother found you."

"Why, Jessi?" he asked, not looking a bit surprised by her confession.

"Because now you don't need Anna Kate or me." From nowhere, tears sprang to Jessi's eyes. Determined that Gabe wouldn't see them, she turned her head.

But he caught her chin in his fingers and gently guided her gaze back to his. "I don't even know those people. Oh, they may be blood kin, all right, but they're still strangers. I need you, babe. I need Anna Kate. You're both a critical part of my life and will be forever. Do you believe me?"

Reassured, at least for the moment, Jessi gave him a smile from the heart. "Yes, and I apologize for projecting my ulterior motives onto you. I think deep inside I was afraid that if given half a chance, I'd use sex to snag you."

Gabe laughed and fell back on the bed, arms outflung. "Go ahead. Make my night!"

"Don't tempt me." Leaning back on the bed, Jessi propped her elbow on the bed and curled close to Gabe's body. "Do you know that if I was on the pill, I'd offer you half my bed right this minute and then share *that* half with you?"

"You would?"

"Yeah."

"To 'snag me'?" He sounded amused by the idea.

Jessi felt her face flush. "No, you're really smarter than that, and I know it."

"Then why?"

"Because I want you so much." Jessi traced the outline of his lips with her forefinger. "I don't suppose you have a condom in your wallet?"

"No...damn the luck."

She mulled over their situation in silence for a moment.

"I guess you could sleep on top of the covers, and I could sleep under them...?"

"Get real."

Jessi sighed again. "Then what do you think we should do?"

"I think we should have wild, abandoned sex all night long."

"And if I get pregnant? We'd have to file the marriage papers, have to make this thing legal, which means commitment. Are you ready for that, Gabe?"

He shrugged as if legal marriage didn't faze him a bit. "So we'll have three kids instead of two. Big fat deal."

Suddenly light-headed with joy, warm with love, Jessi lay her head on Gabe's shoulder. His arm came around her—a cherished embrace.

I love you so much. The thought echoed loudly in Jessi's head, and for one panicked second she thought she'd verbalized it. What would he say if she did? Jessi instantly wondered. Afraid of spoiling this newfound camaraderie, she decided not to find out, instead choosing to slip her hand under his T-shirt and draw lazy circles on his broad chest.

"I suppose I should move Anna Kate in here so you can sleep in your bed."

"I'll do it," Gabe told her, but did not move.

Five minutes slipped by, then ten.

"Are you asleep?" Jessi asked.

"Are you kidding?" Gabe answered, words that reminded her of their steamy idyll in the woods an eternity ago.

Was he reminded, too? she wondered.

The tension in his body told her that he might be.

"Are you going to move Anna Kate?" she asked.

"Yeah."

"When?"

"When I find the willpower to get off this bed."

"There's always later."

"Thanks so much for the encouragement." Gabe sucked in a ragged breath and then sat up.

Reluctantly Jessi let her hand fall away from him. "I'm sure this is for the best."

"I doubt it," he muttered, getting to his feet and walking to the closed bedroom door. Jessi did the same. But instead of opening that door and stepping out, Gabe turned and caught her up in a bone-crushing embrace. His mouth covered hers in a kiss felt clear to Jessi's bare toes. Abruptly breaking that contact, Gabe then raised her sleep shirt. He bent down to nuzzle her breasts, each in turn, before dropping to his knees in front of her.

Gabe tucked his thumbs under the elastic of her bikini panties to pull them down in back, then ran his hands over her hips as he'd done once before—a move every bit as tantalizing as the first time, if not more. He next pressed kisses to her breasts, her stomach, her navel before trailing his lips lower...but only a little.

Clinging to his tense body as she now did, Jessi knew exactly why he stopped there. One wrong move would do it for the both of them, and the morning sun would find two sated lovers instead of responsible adults who knew what was right and always did it.

"Anna Kate?" she reluctantly whispered.

"I'm...going...now," he replied between kisses to each bare breast. He stood and kissed her mouth again, a long, wet kiss that left her weak, then turned sharply, opened the door and left the room.

Jessi staggered into the wall, against which she leaned until she got her breath and balance back. Just as she tugged up her panties, Gabe stepped into the bedroom again, Anna Kate in his arms. Jessi sprang to life, moving to the bed and turning back the covers so he could put the sleeping child there. Once he accomplished that, Jessi pulled the covers up over her daughter and tucked her in.

For several seconds, she stood watching her child sleep. Gabe, standing just behind, wrapped his arms around Jessi, hugged her hard, then left the room, closing the door softly behind him.

Jessi crawled into the bed with her daughter even though she doubted she would sleep. Memories of the day and, in particular, the last half hour ricocheted inside her head, but time and again one special scene came sharply into focus: Gabe's reassuring her that she and Anna Kate would always have a place in his life.

Still worried—foolishly or not—about the effect Gabe's family would have on his need for her and her daughter, Jessi reminded herself that he still needed her money and skill.

And then there was the fact that he wanted her body.

Oh, did that gorgeous man want her body. Jessi knew that well, believed that completely...even if she still had doubts and fears about everything else.

When Jessi awoke the next morning, she felt surprisingly rested and optimistic. Noting that Anna Kate was already up and gone—and probably upset about the switch in beds—Jessi made short work of rising and dressing.

She left the bedroom just ten minutes after waking, only to find herself alone in the trailer. A quick glance at her watch revealed she'd slept until nine o'clock, a rare occurrence. Feeling quite guilty, Jessi peeked out the window and spied her husband and daughter staring up into a tree.

Curious about what they saw, Jessi walked to the door. But just as she reached it, the cell phone buzzed to indicate an incoming call. She couldn't locate the instrument at first, but then found it under a pillow on the love seat and snatched it up.

"Hello."

"Edward Logan Stiles, here. May I speak to Gabriel Dillard."

Jessi's heart sank in spite of all her good intentions and all Gabe's wonderful promises. "I'll get him."

She walked to the door and summoned her husband, who

reached the trailer in three giant steps. Without remorse, Jessi worriedly listened to Gabe's side of the conversation.

"Hello, Mr. Stiles. How are you?" Gabe said into the phone as he slipped into the eating booth. What followed was a very one-sided conversation that told Jessi nothing and reassured her not at all about her precarious, in her opinion, position in his life. "I'm not sure. Could be tomorrow, could be two weeks from now." He listened some more. "What, exactly, are you saying, Mr. Stiles?"

Jessi noted the set of Gabe's jaw, the tension in his neck and shoulders.

"But why would he do this?"

The color drained from Gabe's face. His gaze found Jessi's. He looked shocked, uncertain, and reached out for her. Jessi went to him at once, sliding onto the bench seat, wrapping her arms around his waist even as she lay her head on his shoulder. Gabe put his arm around her.

"I see." He sat in silence, listening intently to whatever else Mr. Edward Logan Stiles had to say. "Yeah. Tell him I'll call." Gabe wrapped a strand of Jessi's hair around his finger. "I understand, and thank you, sir. Goodbye." With the push of a button, Gabe ended the call.

Though tempted to prompt him into an explanation, Jessi did nothing but hold on tight and wait.

"You aren't going to believe this," he finally muttered, still playing with her hair.

"Try me."

"It seems my f-father—" he stumbled over the unfamiliar word "—had money."

Jessi tensed, but said nothing yet.

"Reo...my, um, brother...has money, too. Money of his own."

"So...?"

"He wants no part of our father's money. He intends for me and Mariah to share the entire estate."

"Just how much money are we talking here?" Jessi

asked, slipping out of Gabe's embrace, turning in the seat so she could get a good look at him.

He swallowed hard and gave her a ghost of a smile. "Mr. Stiles couldn't say exactly…I mean, they haven't found my sister or anything… but he said it's a lot. I mean *really a lot.*"

Oh no. The beginning of the end… "I'm thrilled for you, Gabe," she somehow managed to choke out.

Apparently, Gabe wasn't fooled. "You don't look thrilled."

"I really am, I just—"

"What? Think I'm going to dump you for some high society chick?" He laughed at the mere idea.

Jessi wasn't amused. "Exactly."

Gabe's jaw dropped. "I was just kidding."

"Well, I'm not. Now that you've got a family and a fortune, what do you need me for?" She slid out of the booth and turned to face him. "Cooks are a dime a dozen. And sex…well, money buys that, too. That's all we have between us, Gabe. *What do you need me for?*"

Clearly stunned, Gabe just stared at her. "You are one insecure lady."

"Yeah…and I have a damn good reason."

"Then could you please just share it, because I'm having a hell of a time understanding why it's so hard for you to believe me when I say I want to be with you and Anna Kate—"

At the mention of her daughter's name, Jessi whirled around and bolted to the door. Too many minutes had passed since she'd last checked on her four-year-old, way too many minutes even for a child who'd always played responsibly.

The girl was not in sight.

"Anna Kate?" Jessi called, scanning the campsite.

By now Gabe stood behind her. He added his booming bass call. "Anna Kate!"

When she did not reply, Jessi leapt out of the trailer with

Gabe on her heels. He strode to where Anna Kate had been playing and knelt to study the rain-soaked ground. His gaze followed the path they'd forged yesterday, a path that led into the trees. He spat out a curse and leapt to his feet.

"The creek," he told Jessi. "She's gone to the creek."

"Oh my God."

"Mommy! Mommy!"

Terror froze Jessi to the spot, but Gabe charged into the woods.

Chapter Twelve

It wasn't that far to the creek, but it felt like a mile by the time Jessi stumbled to a halt at the water's edge, breathless and terrified. Neither Gabe nor Anna Kate could be seen in the water, so she turned and scanned the autumn foliage for them.

"Jessi! Over here!"

Jessi barely heard those words over the roar of the water, but spun at once toward the sound. Just north, behind a tangle of brambles, she spied Anna Kate, sitting on a rock, and Gabe, on his knees beside her.

Jessi burst into tears of relief, and, blinded by those tears, tripped over a stump in her haste to get to her daughter. Gabe reached her in a flash, helped her up and disentangled her clothing from the greedy brambles.

"She's all right, Jessi. She's all right," he told her, almost shouting to be heard.

Jessi barely managed a nod.

After wiping away her tears with the hem of his flannel shirt, Gabe took Jessi's hand in his and led her to Anna Kate who sobbed uncontrollably.

"What's wrong, honey?" Jessi asked, sitting on the rock beside the four-year-old and hugging her tight. She said the words right into the child's ear so she could hear.

"M-m-y b-b-bear." Anna Kate pointed to the rushing water.

"Why'd you bring him here?" Jessi asked, instantly guessing the stuffed toy had met with a tragic end. "You know you aren't supposed to go out of sight of camp."

"But h-he wanted to see how high the w-water came."

Jessi, almost nauseous with relief, glanced up at Gabe, only then noting how shaken he appeared. His eyes glinted suspiciously, too, almost as if he'd shed tears of his own.

But tears meant love. And Gabe didn't love them.

Did he?

"I'll look for him," the man in question abruptly announced, beginning a hike further downstream along the water's edge. Jessi and Anna Kate watched until he disappeared from view behind a stand of young ponderosa pines.

"Are you s-sorry 'bout my b-bear?" asked Anna Kate.

"Not half as sorry as I'd have been if it was you and not that silly, willy bear floating down the creek." Jessi slipped off the rock and knelt down in front of her daughter, eye level. "I love you so much, honey. You scared me to death. Please, please don't ever do that again."

"That's what Daddy G s-said."

"So he told you not to do it again, too, huh?"

"Not that part." She sniffed and swiped at her tears. "H-he said he loved me, and I scared him."

"Oh." Startled by this piece of news, Jessi could do nothing more than sit in silence to analyze it.

Gabe loved Anna Kate.

Well, who wouldn't? she immediately berated herself, eyeing her beautiful daughter. Such love didn't mean a thing, really. And affection for the child didn't necessarily mean affection for the mom, either.

Just then, Anna Kate squealed and pointed, then jumped

off the rock. Catching her daughter by the hem of her purple shirt, Jessi turned and saw Gabe coming back upstream with the dripping teddy bear held high overhead. Jessi noted that his jeans were wet clear up to the bottom of the button fly; it looked as if he'd actually waded that wild water to save the bear.

Merciful heavens!

Only when mere steps separated the two females from Gabe did Jessi let her daughter go. At once, Anna Kate ran to her stepdad and threw her arms around his legs.

"Watch out!" he exclaimed. "I'm wet as this bear." He handed her the sodden toy.

"Thank you! Thank you!" Anna Kate sang, clearly not minding Gabe's or her bear's soaked state. She held the stuffed animal in front of her and shook a finger at him. "You silly, willy bear!"

"Is that his name now?" Gabe teased. "Silly Willy?"

Anna Kate's eyes, still swimming in tears, lit up. "Yes," she announced and then hugged her precious Silly Willy so hard that she squeezed a stream of creek water out of him.

Jessi's gaze found Gabe's. Her heart swelled with undeniable love, and leaning close, she kissed him gently on the lips. "Thanks."

"My pleasure," he solemnly answered.

Together, the three of them walked back to the camp, where they found that their employers had come back and now waited for them.

"It's Shari!" exclaimed Anna Kate running ahead. She showed both the adults her bear and probably told them about his swim, if Shari's immediate look of horror was anything to judge by. Anna Kate, clearly none the worse for her adventure, then ran indoors, no doubt to get a towel for Silly Willy.

Shari smiled rather sheepishly when August and Jessi reached her seconds later. "Sorry about running out on you guys yesterday and about leaving you without wheels last night.''

"As you can see,'' Jessi answered. "We made it just fine except for a little dip in the creek.'' She indicated Gabe's soaked jeans. "I think you and August needed the time alone to clear the air. You did clear the air, didn't you?'' She glanced anxiously from one to the other of her bosses.

"We did,'' August answered.

A quick study of his face revealed that a heretofore unseen twinkle now lighted his eye. He looked relaxed, happy—expressions barely glimpsed before now. Jessi smiled and glanced at Gabe, who must have noted the same things. At any rate, he gave her a quick don't-you-just-love-it? wink.

"And now we have an announcement to make...actually, two announcements.'' August glanced at his wife. "Do you want to tell them, or shall I?''

"You do it,'' she answered with a decidedly smug smile.

"We're going to have a baby,'' he said.

"The reason I've been so uptight,'' Shari quickly added, taking Jessi's hand. "I wanted to tell you, but I couldn't until I knew how August felt about it. Then he was such a grump, I was afraid to tell *him*.''

It was August's turn to smile sheepishly.

"Congratulations,'' Gabe said. "When are you due?''

"April,'' August said. "She's already eight weeks along.''

"You're going to be wonderful parents,'' said Jessi, hugging first Shari and then her husband.

"Yeah,'' echoed Gabe, shaking August's hand, then slapping him on the back. "Couldn't have happened to a nicer couple.''

"Yeah, well, you might not think I'm so nice when you hear my other announcement.'' August, looking uncharacteristically uncertain, glanced to his wife for encouragement.

"Just spit it out, Gus," she advised, much to Jessi's and Gabe's amusement.

He did. "I've finally realized what you two have probably known all along—this treasure hunt is a waste of everyone's time. My motives for it were never right. And now that Shari's convinced me she loves me for what I am, not what I have, was or even may be, I've lost the need to prove anything." His gaze met Gabe's. "I'll still pay you, of course. I, um, hope this isn't too much of an inconvenience. I mean, you did get married just to please me...."

"Something we'd probably have done anyway," Gabe said. "If we'd met, that is...."

"Excuse me?" August's gaze nailed Gabe to the spot even as Jessi's heart flipped over backwards—at least that's what it felt like.

"Since you've come clean with us, I think it's time for us to come clean with you." Gabe glanced at Jessi. "Don't you?"

What was she supposed to do now? Say no? Seriously doubting the wisdom of true confessions just then, Jessi could only gulp and nod.

"Jessi and I had never met before Elaina introduced us, just over a week ago."

"B-but—" Shari, wide-eyed, couldn't even finish her stammered response.

August didn't have that problem. "You're kidding, right?"

"I'm afraid not," Gabe answered.

Clearly doubting that answer, August looked to Jessi for confirmation.

She just shrugged.

"You were planning to get a divorce later?" August appeared puzzled—no big surprise. The whole temporary marriage thing sounded foolish, money or no.

"An annulment, actually," Jessi told him. "But we never filed the papers, so we aren't really married. Oh, we were going to, but then we realized we could save ourselves some legal fees…I'm really sorry.''

Shari waved away the apology. "So that's why Gabe slept in the little bed. I did wonder.'' The next instant, she looked mortified. Jessi guessed she'd just remembered the birthday present, but Shari simply clamped her mouth shut and said not another word.

Gabe cleared his throat rather noisily. "I know it wasn't particularly scrupulous, but I needed the money and so did Jessi.''

"Hey,'' August said, holding up a hand to halt further explanation. "I don't deserve an explanation, and I don't even want one. I will say it's hard to believe two people so perfectly matched really aren't.'' He shook his head in disbelief.

"*That's* sure the truth,'' Shari murmured with a shake of her head.

Gabe laughed. "We've discussed that very thing ourselves, actually.''

"And…?'' Clearly, the blonde hoped for a fairy-tale ending to the Gabe and Jessi love story.

Well, so did Jessi.

"And we're going to spend some more time together to get to know one another better, aren't we?'' Gabe lay an arm across Jessi's shoulders in a casual hug.

Somehow Jessi managed a weak, "Yes.'' They were, indeed, going to spend time together: packing up…driving home…. After that, who really knew? Certainly not Jessi Dillard-soon-to-be-Landers again, who, at the moment, couldn't bear to think about her uncertain future at all.

After a little more catching up, August proposed they celebrate their last night together with a cookout. He even had steaks, picked up while in town. Since it wasn't raining at the moment, everyone enthusiastically agreed to the plan.

Dinner proved to be fun and late, thanks to their efforts to pack up what they could while it was still daylight. Finally, at eight o'clock, they sat around a table in the food tent to eat steaks and french fries. For dessert, Jessi served quick peach cobbler, made from an old recipe of her mother's.

Anna Kate yawned all during the meal, so when she finished eating, Jessi hustled her and her doll off to bed. Silly Willy, his ears pinned to a makeshift clothesline in the bedroom, hung around. August and Shari soon vanished indoors too, which left Jessi and Gabe alone. Though tempted to sit outside for a while longer, they didn't. The evening breeze blew cool and a little too damp, thanks to the overabundance of moisture everywhere.

Once inside the kitchen of their trailer, Gabe helped Jessi with the few dishes—they'd used mostly disposable plates and cutlery that night. He washed for a change, while she rinsed and dried.

Jessi noted that he seemed to be in no hurry, but couldn't imagine why until he finally revealed the reason.

"You never answered my question today, Jessi."

"And which question was that?"

"I asked you why you were so insecure about us. You said there was a good reason, but then never shared it with me. Care to now?"

How could she answer without revealing her heart? Jessi wondered. He'd never so much as hinted he returned her affection. He'd even agreed with her when she had said *not* loving each other was a good thing.

"I'm insecure because we don't love each other," Jessi finally blurted. "Oh, I know you said love just complicated things, but I keep thinking how hard it is to tolerate someone you do care about. How on earth will two people who don't love each other ever stay together when the going gets tough?"

Gabe, standing with his hands suspended over the sink and dripping sudsy water, didn't say a word.

"Are you listening, Gabe?" She threw down her dish towel and grabbed his arm, tugging on it until he turned to face her.

"I'm listening," he finally answered, his gaze steady, his hands and forearms now dripping soap on the floor.

"Then tell me how. I have to know."

Gabe hesitated another moment before replying. "I've been thinking about what I said, and I'm not sure I was right."

Jessi caught her breath. "What do you mean?"

"What if I told you I haven't been totally honest? What if I said I loved you? Would you feel better then?"

"Only if you really meant it," she answered, her stomach in knots, her pulse pounding in her throat. "Do you, Gabe?" She caught him by the biceps and peered deeply into his clear blue eyes. "Do you?"

"I believe I do," he softly replied. "Do you...love me?"

Jessi smiled at his hesitancy. "I believe I do."

Gabe's shoulders sagged. He let out his pent-up breath in a long, slow sigh. Only then did Jessi suspect the enormity of his relief. His hard hug confirmed it.

She cherished the sensation of Gabe's arms—his wet, soapy arms—wrapped so tightly around her. This was good. This was right. This was destiny.

This was also forever, and suddenly Jessi's chaotic world became orderly and secure.

"Mommy! Come quick!"

Certain her daughter had dreamed again about spiders or perhaps just the creek, Jessi slipped free of Gabe's embrace, snatched up a lantern, and hurried to the bedroom. He followed on her heels.

"What is it?" Jessi demanded of Anna Kate, now sitting up in bed. "What's wrong?" She walked around one side of the bed; Gabe walked around the other.

"Silly Willy wet the bed," her daughter replied with a look of feigned innocence at her mother and then her stepfather.

Inspection of the sheets revealed that the thoroughly-soaked bear—who'd mysteriously climbed down from the

clothesline and crawled into bed next to Anna Kate—now
lay in a puddle.

Jessi groaned. Gabe chuckled. Anna Kate put a hand over
her mouth and giggled impishly.

The remarkably good-natured adults—love does have a
way of making life fun—made short work of changing the
bed linens and hanging Silly Willy back on the clothesline,
where all bad bears, especially waterlogged ones, had *better*
stay.

"I love you," Gabe said to his stepdaughter once he'd
tucked her in again.

"Love you." She echoed the critical words as if that
wonderful man had said them every night of her short life.

"And *I* love you," Jessi told Anna Kate.

"Love *you*, too," the child once again echoed with a
telltale yawn.

Seconds later, Jessi and Gabe stepped out of the bedroom
and softly closed the door. Gabe led Jessi right by the un-
finished dishes to the love seat, turning off each lantern as
they passed it. Once seated, he turned the lamp Jessi still
held way down, then set it on the table and coaxed her into
his lap. For long moments, he held her close in the shadows
without speaking.

"Are bedtimes always this exciting when you've got a
kid around?" Gabe finally murmured, his words warm
against her skin.

Jessi laughed softly and smoothed an errant lock of hair
back from his forehead. "You call that exciting? Just wait
until Ryder joins us."

"I'm asking a lot of you, aren't I?" Gabe murmured
with a shake of his head. "I mean, he's not even your kid,
yet I'm expecting you to take him in and raise him."

She arched an eyebrow at him. "You think I'm asking
less for Anna Kate?"

"But I feel like she's mine."

"And I'll feel the same about Ryder." Jessi now ran a
finger over his cheek and chin, already rough with a new

growth of whiskers. "You know, old Silas had the right idea when he called those family photos 'treasure.' Obviously he knew what matters most."

"Amen to that," Gabe answered, adding, "God, I love you," the most precious words Jessi had ever heard.

"No doubts?" she asked.

"None at all."

"Good, because I love you, too."

"No doubts?" he echoed with a grin.

"Not even one," Jessi told him, adding, "It's going to be okay, isn't it?"

"No, ma'am," Gabe answered. "It's going to be perfect."

Vroooom. Vroooom.

"That's right! You're doing it!"

Gabe grinned with pleasure at Ryder's shouts of encouragement—shouts intended for Anna Kate, just learning to handle her brand-new remote-controlled race car. Ryder, with them for a Thanksgiving visit, had brought the car as a hello gift for his soon-to-be stepsister.

Their proud "papa" sat on his Yakima, Washington, park bench and marveled that the two kids tolerated each other so well. Six years and gender separated them, after all. But then most youngsters had the knack of accepting change easily—a knack for which Gabe would've swapped his Snake River spread at that moment.

As if sensing his nervousness, Jessi, now his legal wife, reached out and patted his thigh.

"You're going to be fine," she told him, throwing in a sweet smile of encouragement for good measure.

"Yeah, sure," Gabe agreed. He could not manage a smile himself. Too many emotions—curiosity, angst and anticipation among them—now formed a giant knot in his stomach. His hands actually trembled and sweat beaded his brow even though the clouds spit snow.

Waiting to meet his half brother for the first time was

proving to be more damned stressful than getting married, and *that* had nearly killed him.

But look how well everything turned out.

Jessi chose that moment to jump up and grab Anna Kate's car, which careened precariously close to an elderly couple sitting on another bench just down the sidewalk. After setting the vehicle where it couldn't hit or run over anyone's toes, Jessi walked back to their bench.

Gabe watched the way the breeze rustled her hair, which hung loose today. He noted with appreciation her easy stride, the sway of her hips, the totally-female bounce of her breasts, barely visible under her cotton sweater and light jacket. Her smile, her bright eyes…everything about her completed the picture of perfect health, of homespun beauty.

And she belongs to me, he thought, experiencing the usual quickening of his pulse, the sexual tensing of his body, the warmth of love and pride.

Gabe held out his arm to his wife, who slipped under it to cuddle close to him on the bench.

"You know what would be even more fun than meeting my brother right now?" he asked.

"Almost anything?" She tipped her head back so she could meet his gaze.

Gabe had to laugh at her clever guess. "Actually I was going to suggest that we slip off behind a bush somewhere and play birds and bees."

"Mmm. You're a real nature boy, aren't you?"

He grinned. "Bingo."

"And what about Anna Kate and Ryder?"

"We'll hire those senior citizens to baby-sit them." He kissed the top of Jessi's head.

"If that man getting out of that car over there is who I think he is, we might be able to hire him, instead, and for a family rate."

Gabe jerked his head up to look where she pointed.

"Lordy, Gabe, he looks so much like you! Or do you look like him?"

Gabe didn't answer. All he could do was stare at the tall, dark-haired man now in earnest conversation with a slender redhead. The man—almost certainly his half brother, Reo Sampson—glanced his way, then said something else to the woman, who caught him by the arms, turned him to face the park, and gave him a gentle shove in Gabe's direction.

That proof of Reo's uncertainty did wonders to ease Gabe's own nervousness. Mesmerized by the sight of an honest-to-goodness blood relative, he could only stare as the man squared his shoulders and began to walk toward him.

How should I greet him? Treat him?

Reo chose that moment to smile broadly at Gabe, and his quickened step seemed to say he'd overcome his jitters and couldn't wait to be face-to-face with his newfound kin. At once, joy filled Gabe, replacing all other emotion. He leapt to his feet and strode to meet his brother, who offered him his right hand.

"You've got to be Gabriel. I'm Reo," he said as he took, shook and released Gabe's hand.

Suddenly choked up, Gabe couldn't even answer for a moment. Embarrassed, he blinked back the moisture in his eyes, then shook his head in disbelief at his roller-coaster emotions. "Sorry. I've been a nervous wreck all morning."

Reo chuckled softly. "I can relate to that." Looking over his shoulder, he motioned for the redhead to join them. She came at once, swiping at tears as she walked. Reo retrieved a handkerchief from his pocket and handed it to her.

"Gabriel, this is my wife, Rusty. Rusty, meet my—" Reo's gaze locked with Gabe's; he grinned from ear to ear "—brother."

Rusty surprised Gabe with a hug instead of a handshake. "I'm so glad you agreed to see us today, Gabriel—" She swiped a stray tear.

"Gabe."

"Gabe," Rusty obediently repeated with a smile. She glanced over his shoulder. "Is that your wife?"

Gabe shook off his emotional daze and waved Jessi over.

"Sorry," he apologized again, this time to his patient spouse. He introduced her to Rusty and Reo. An awkward silence fell over the group. Rusty nudged Reo with her elbow.

"Right, um, well, we've got a lot to talk about. I'll tell you now that we have a lead on Mariah. The P.I. I hired thinks she's somewhere in Texas. I'm sure you have a million other questions. Want to talk here or go to my hotel suite?"

"How about your suite?" Jessi softly suggested since Gabe didn't offer an answer.

His thoughts stayed on his twin. Gut feeling told him Reo was right and she lived in Texas. That meant it wouldn't be long until he met her, too.

"The hotel has video games or movies we can rent for the kids," Rusty said, her gaze on Ryder and Anna Kate, still racing their cars a short distance away. "And I'll keep an eye on them so you three can talk."

"Why, thank you," Jessi answered.

"Rusty's great with kids," Reo said. "In fact, that's how we met. The director of the day care in my building hired her to give a Mardi Gras party. We got stuck on an elevator together."

"How romantic," Jessi murmured.

"Actually, it wasn't. She had all these kids wearing weird costumes with her."

Gabe and Jessi laughed. "Sounds as crazy as the way we met," Gabe told them.

"And where exactly was that?" Rusty asked, her curiosity clearly piqued.

"At our wedding," Gabe answered, at their shocked expressions adding, "It's a long story that I'd better tell later."

"Later..." Reo said the word slowly, almost as if he

savored it and the future it stood for. His steady gaze locked with Gabe's. "My father made a bad mistake. I know I can't turn back time or ever make things right with your mother, but I swear to you now that I'm going to do my level best to make sure you and Mariah get everything that should've been yours."

"Do you know very much about my mother?"

"Well, I can tell you that she made her living as a psychic working in New Orleans. Met my, er, *our* father when he visited there once he got out of the service."

Gabe laughed softly at that news of his mother's profession, which explained so very much. He felt Jessi slip her arm around his waist and gave her a quick smile.

"Stiles told me he mentioned Dad's estate when he talked to you," Reo continued. "Did he tell you how much it's worth?"

"Doesn't matter," Gabe said, words from the heart. At Reo's look of surprise, he added, "Oh, money's great, don't get me wrong, but what I care about most in this world can't even be bought."

"Your family?" asked Rusty Sampson with a loving glace at her husband, who gave her back a wink.

"Bingo!" Gabe and Jessi agreed together.

Though the topic of conversation soon changed, Gabe's thoughts lingered on the miracle of his family. Who'd have believed a loner like himself could transform so painlessly into a husband, a dad, a brother? But he had, and he would never stop marveling at the change.

Jessi was now as vital to life as the air he breathed, Gabe realized, his gaze consuming her. As though she felt the heated look, his wife turned and gave him a smile that took his breath away even as it reassured him that he didn't need to fear this power she held over him. Jessi belonged to him for keeps, just as he belonged to her.

Forever was theirs to cherish.

* * * * *

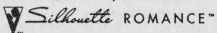

Take 2 bestselling love stories FREE

Plus get a FREE surprise gift!

Special Limited-Time Offer

Mail to Silhouette Reader Service™

3010 Walden Avenue
P.O. Box 1867
Buffalo, N.Y. 14240-1867

YES! Please send me 2 free Silhouette Romance™ novels and my free surprise gift. Then send me 6 brand-new novels every month, which I will receive months before they appear in bookstores. Bill me at the low price of $2.90 each plus 25¢ delivery and applicable sales tax, if any.* That's the complete price, and a saving of over 10% off the cover prices—quite a bargain! I understand that accepting the books and gift places me under no obligation ever to buy any books. I can always return a shipment and cancel at any time. Even if I never buy another book from Silhouette, the 2 free books and the surprise gift are mine to keep forever.

215 SEN CH7S

Name	(PLEASE PRINT)	
Address	Apt. No.	
City	State	Zip

This offer is limited to one order per household and not valid to present Silhouette Romance™ subscribers. *Terms and prices are subject to change without notice. Sales tax applicable in N.Y.

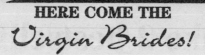

MATERNITY LEAVE

Coming September 1998

Three delightful stories about the blessings
and surprises of "Labor" Day.

TABLOID BABY by Candace Camp

She was whisked to the hospital in the nick of time....

THE NINE-MONTH KNIGHT
by Cait London

A down-on-her-luck secretary is experiencing
odd little midnight cravings....

THE PATERNITY TEST by Sherryl Woods

The stick turned blue before her
biological clock struck twelve....

*These three special women are very pregnant...and very
single, although they won't be either for too much longer,
because baby—and Daddy—are on their way!*

Available at your favorite retail outlet.

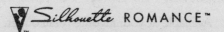